The Lost Journal's of Fitzwilliam Darcy

June Calva

Published by June Calva, 2024.

This is a work of fiction. Similarities to real people, places, or events are entirely coincidental.

THE LOST JOURNAL'S OF FITZWILLIAM DARCY

First edition. April 22, 2024.

ISBN: 979-8224481910

Written by June Calva.

July 18, 1811

In the grandeur of Pemberley's drawing room, suffused with the gentle light of a summer's afternoon, I find myself reflecting upon a conversation most pivotal—a dialogue that may very well chart the course of my immediate future. Charles Bingley, a gentleman whose spirits are as buoyant as mine are restrained, has proffered an invitation most unexpected. He wishes for me to accompany him to Hertfordshire, where he contemplates the leasing of an estate known as Netherfield Park. His request, delivered with a candidness that is his signature, prompts a contemplation of the serenity I so cherish here at Pemberley against the stirrings of curiosity for the venture he proposes.

As we sat amongst the rich tapestries and ancestral portraits that adorn my family's home, Charles, with an earnestness that belies his usual levity, spoke of Netherfield. "Darcy, my friend," he began with a characteristic lack of preamble, "I have received word of a property that promises to be most advantageous for a man of my situation. Netherfield Park, they call it. I am most eager to make your acquaintance with it and would value your esteemed opinion on its merits."

I must confess, his entreaty caught me somewhat unawares. The notion of departing the tranquility of Derbyshire for the unknown precincts of Hertfordshire was not one I had entertained. Yet the sincerity in Charles's gaze, the unabashed hopefulness, compelled me to consider his request with an open heart.

"The country has charms that the city cannot match," I conceded, my gaze drifting towards the verdant expanse visible from the window. "When do you intend to undertake this venture?"

"With all due haste," Charles declared, his gaze following mine to the landscape beyond. "I would set out within the month, should that suit your convenience."

The idea of casting aside the familiar embrace of my ancestral home, even temporarily, gave me a moment's pause. Pemberley is more than mere bricks and mortar; it is a testament to the Darcy legacy—a legacy I uphold with all the gravity my station demands. Yet the prospect of aiding a friend in a matter of such import weighed heavily upon my decision.

"You have my word, Bingley. I shall accompany you to Hertfordshire," I affirmed, offering him a nod of assent. "Your enthusiasm is persuasive, and I would be remiss in my duties as a friend were I to decline."

A broad smile broke across Charles's countenance, his relief palpable. "Your company shall make the journey all the more agreeable," he replied, the warmth of his friendship a balm to my often solitary existence.

Our discussion then turned to the practicalities of our impending excursion—the procurement of conveyance, the arrangements for our stay, and the manifold considerations such an undertaking necessitates. Charles spoke of the assembly balls and other such social engagements with a fervor I could not match, though I humored him with attentive nods. His mention of the local society, of the families and daughters we were likely to encounter, was met with a measure of reserve on my part. For while Charles may entertain thoughts of romance and companionship, I remain steadfast in my belief that such intimacies are to be entered into with the utmost discernment.

As the sun dipped below the horizon, casting the room into the soft glow of twilight, Charles took his leave, his spirits buoyed by our plans. I was left to my solitude, the weight of the day's discussion settling upon my shoulders. Would this change of scenery prove a welcome diversion, or would it merely serve to underscore the differences between Charles's disposition and my own?

In the quiet hours of the night, I commit these thoughts to paper, a record of the turning point that may lead me down a path untrodden.

My life, thus far measured and predictable, stands on the cusp of transformation—whether for weal or woe, the passage of time shall reveal.

Fitzwilliam Darcy

August 5, 1811

The morning dawned with the soft blush of summer as Charles and I embarked upon our journey to Netherfield. Our conveyance, a sturdy coach drawn by four of the finest horses in my stables, rolled steadily through the verdant countryside of Derbyshire. The air, fresh and invigorating, carried with it the promise of new ventures as we left the familiar embrace of Pemberley behind.

Charles was a portrait of eager anticipation, his countenance alight with the prospect of what lay ahead. I, in contrast, maintained a semblance of the composure that is my wont, though internally, I could not deny a certain intrigue at the thought of viewing this estate which had so captured my friend's imagination.

Our conversation during the journey was a blend of practical matters and Charles's buoyant projections for his potential new home. He spoke of the improvements he might undertake, the fetes he could host, and the felicity he envisaged in establishing his own domain. I offered counsel where appropriate, advising caution and due diligence—a balancing voice to his sanguine expectations.

The hours passed with the rolling landscape, our coach carrying us through hamlets and past fields ripe with the season's bounty. We spoke little of the society we might encounter in Hertfordshire, though I was aware of the undercurrent of Charles's hope for congenial companionship. As for myself, I entertained no such aspirations, content in the company of my own thoughts and the solace of a good book.

As the day waned, the silhouette of Netherfield Park rose against the horizon—a vision of Georgian symmetry nestled amidst groves of ancient trees. The estate, though lacking the grandeur of Pemberley, possessed a charm that was undeniable. It was a fitting residence for a gentleman of Charles's means and temperament.

Upon our arrival, we were greeted by the agent, Mr. Morris, a man whose obsequious manner belied an astute mind for business. He ushered us through the entrance hall and into the heart of the manor, where the late afternoon sun cast golden hues across the polished floors.

Charles's delight was palpable as he surveyed each room, his imagination already furnishing them with the laughter and conversation of future gatherings. I followed his lead, my observations more reserved, taking note of the structural integrity, the quality of the craftsmanship, and the practicalities of maintaining such an estate.

Dinner was a quiet affair, the fatigue of travel lending a subdued air to our repast. Yet, even as we dined, Charles's mind was alight with plans for Netherfield, his conversation a monologue of aspirations for the life he might lead here.

As I retired to my chamber for the night, the stillness of the house enveloped me. Netherfield, with its unspoken potential, stood as a blank canvas upon which Charles might paint the future he so ardently desired. And while my presence here was that of advisor and confidant, I could not shake the sense that this journey might herald changes beyond the leasing of an estate.

In the quiet hours of reflection, I penned this entry, capturing the nuances of a day that might prove more consequential than I had first surmised. Tomorrow, we shall further explore Netherfield and its environs, and in doing so, perhaps also uncover new facets of our own characters.

For now, I remain, as always, a man of circumspection, standing on the threshold of the unknown—a position both daunting and, in rare moments of candor, exhilarating.

Fitzwilliam Darcy

August 6, 1811

Upon this day, I have witnessed an event of considerable moment in the life of my friend Charles Bingley—a gentleman whose vivacious spirit is only matched by the generosity of his heart. With an air of solemnity befitting the occasion, he has bound himself to the estate of Netherfield Park, taking upon his shoulders the mantle of a country squire with an enthusiasm that I find both endearing and mildly concerning.

The morning was greeted with a haste uncharacteristic of Pemberley, as we broke our fast amidst the flurry of preparations for our meeting with Mr. Morris. Charles, unable to contain his fervor, spoke in animated tones of his vision for Netherfield. "Darcy, think of it! The balls, the sport, the society! Netherfield shall be a beacon of hospitality in Hertfordshire," he proclaimed with a smile that threatened to split his face.

I met his excitement with a tempered nod, my own thoughts a tangled skein of pride and trepidation. "Indeed, Charles, it is a fine endeavor you embark upon. But I urge you to proceed with caution; an estate is not merely a stage for entertainments but a responsibility that demands dedication and sound judgment."

Charles waved away my counsel with a dismissive hand, his confidence unshaken. "Oh, Darcy, ever the pragmatist! I value your wisdom, but today, let us not dwell on the burdensome. Today, we celebrate the future!"

The hour of our appointment arrived, and we were ushered into Mr. Morris's study—a room lined with shelves of leather-bound ledgers and the faint scent of beeswax. The lease lay before us, a testament to the gravity of the undertaking. Charles, with a hand untroubled by doubt, affixed his signature to the document.

As I watched the ink dry, I could not help but reflect on the path that had led us to this juncture. The carefree days of our youth seemed distant now, as Charles stepped into a role that would define his standing in society. I stood by his side, lending my own signature as a witness to this pivotal moment.

"Congratulations, Mr. Bingley," Mr. Morris intoned with a measured smile. "Netherfield Park is let at last, it is now yours."

Charles beamed with pride. "Thank you, Mr. Morris. I assure you, Netherfield and its lands shall be well cared for under my stewardship."

As the day waned, Charles busied himself with the myriad tasks that ownership entailed, his earlier excitement giving way to a focus that was both necessary and reassuring. I, in turn, took to exploring the estate's confines, the expanse of its lawns, and the serenity of its gardens offering a momentary reprieve from the weight of change.

Returning to the manor as dusk approached, I found Charles deep in conversation with the housekeeper, his voice carrying through the halls. "We shall need additional staff, of course. And the drawing-room—the draperies are in dire need of replacement. Oh, and be sure the cellars are well-stocked. We are to be exemplary hosts, after all!"

I retired to my room, the day's events swirling in my mind as I penned this entry. The conviction with which Charles embraced his new role was admirable, yet it served as a reminder of the solitude that often accompanied my own position. Netherfield was to be a place of gathering, of society—a stark contrast to the quiet dignity of Pemberley.

It is in these quiet hours that I find myself wrestling with the notion of change. Change, that inexorable force that shapes our lives in ways both subtle and profound. For Charles, change is an adventure to be seized; for me, it is a specter to be examined from every angle.

As I set my quill aside, the silence of Netherfield envelopes me. It is a silence that speaks of potential, of beginnings, of the myriad paths that lay open before us. And in that silence, I find a challenge—a challenge to step beyond the boundaries of my own reticence and to embrace the unknown with a measure of grace.

Fitzwilliam Darcy

August 18, 1811

It has been but twelve days since Charles assumed the mantle of a country gentleman, and already Netherfield is abuzz with the stirrings of a burgeoning social calendar. Today's entry, I must note, is punctuated by a series of visits from the neighbourhood's gentlemen, who, upon learning of Charles's arrival, deemed it proper to make his acquaintance and welcome him into the fold of Hertfordshire society.

The morning was filled with a parade of local landowners and their sons, each eager to assess the man who had taken up residence in the estate that had stood untenanted for some time. Charles, of course, was in his element, greeting each visitor with the grace and charm that is his custom. I found myself in the role of observer, content to watch the proceedings from a respectful remove.

Amongst the visitors was a Mr. Bennet, of the nearby Longbourn estate—a gentleman of an age with my own father, had he still been with us. His countenance bore the marks of intelligence and an understated wit that caught me somewhat off guard. He approached with an ease and lack of ceremony that spoke to a character unconcerned with the trappings of wealth or status.

"Mr. Bingley, I presume?" he inquired, extending a hand that Charles shook with enthusiasm.

Charles greeted our visitor with the warmth he bestows upon all, "Indeed, sir, and may I say what a pleasure it is to receive you," his smile broad and genuine.

Mr. Bennet was ensconced in an armchair by the hearth, a cup of tea in hand. His eyes, sharp and discerning, swept the room before settling on me with a curiosity I could not readily discern. I admit, I was taken aback by the directness of his gaze—a trait so seldom encountered in the polished veneer of London society.

His gaze lingered on me for a moment, discerning, before he offered a slight smile. "I am told you possess a discerning eye for the finer points of estate management, Mr. Darcy. I trust Netherfield meets with your approval?"

"It is a fine estate, indeed," I allowed, noting the subtle probing within his question.

Conversation flowed as the tea was poured, and Mr. Bennet spoke of Longbourn and his family with a wit so dry it threatened to desiccate the very air we breathed. He regaled us with tales of his daughters, each anecdote tinged with a sarcasm so subtle it was almost imperceptible. Yet, beneath the veil of his humor, I sensed a depth of affection for his offspring.

Charles, ever eager to discuss the impending assembly, sought Mr. Bennet's counsel on the matter. The older gentleman assured him of the neighborhood's anticipation and, with a wry smile, hinted at the excitement his daughters held for the event. I sensed in Charles a kindling of interest, spurred no doubt by the prospect of engaging with the fairer sex—a pursuit I find more taxing than exhilarating.

The conversation turned then to the topic of the surrounding lands, the recent harvest, and the expectations for the hunting season. Mr. Bennet spoke with an understated confidence that belied his modest attire, his observations on rural life both insightful and tinged with a dry humour that I could not help but appreciate.

As the hour waned and Mr. Bennet prepared to take his leave, I found myself reflecting on the man's character. He possesses an intellect that is at once both piercing and playful, a combination that intrigues me despite my reservations. His daughters, if they inherit but a fraction of their father's wit, may indeed prove to be society of a different sort than I am accustomed to.

Charles extended an invitation for Mr. Bennet to join us for dinner—an offer that was accepted with a gracious nod. "I look forward to it, Mr. Bingley. It will be a pleasure to introduce you to the rest of my family, in turn."

Upon his departure, Charles turned to me, a gleam of satisfaction in his eye. "Well, Darcy, what think you of our neighbour?"

"He possesses a keen mind," I replied, "and a manner that is refreshingly devoid of pretension."

Charles clapped a hand on my shoulder, his laughter ringing out. "Just so! I do declare, Hertfordshire may yet prove to be a source of great amusement."

The remainder of the day passed in similar fashion, with more of the local gentry coming to pay their respects. It was a veritable study in the breadth of country society—from the overly earnest Mr. Jones, who spoke at length of his prized pig, to the taciturn Sir William Lucas, whose every utterance seemed measured for effect.

As the evening draws in, and I retire to reflect upon the day's encounters, I am struck by the realisation that my initial hesitations regarding our sojourn to Netherfield may have been misplaced. The simplicity of country society, with its lack of artifice and the forthrightness of its inhabitants, is a refreshing change from the often stifling circles of London ton.

Yet, amidst this newfound appreciation, I am mindful of the challenges that lie ahead. The impending assembly looms large in my thoughts—a social occasion that will demand engagement on a level I am seldom comfortable with. I am resolved, however, to support Charles in his endeavours and to navigate the forthcoming events with as much grace as I can muster.

In this quiet hour of night, with only the scratch of my quill for company, I am reminded that life, much like the land we steward, is subject to the seasons of change. May I weather the coming autumn with the same steadfastness that the oaks of Pemberley have shown for generations.

Fitzwilliam Darcy

August 22, 1811

Today's entry is marked by a sense of expectation, a narrative of events relayed to me through the buoyant words of Charles Bingley, for I did not accompany him on his visit to Longbourn—an obligation of courtesy to return the civility extended to us by Mr. Bennet. My own inclinations led me to remain at Netherfield, indulging in the solitude that I so often find to be a balm to my disposition.

Charles departed after breakfast with a liveliness in his step, the prospect of making the acquaintance of Mr. Bennet's reputedly charming daughters evidently occupying his every thought. "Darcy, are you certain you will not join me?" he asked, a note of disappointment in his voice, as he prepared to depart.

I offered him a smile, albeit a restrained one. "I have matters here that require my attention, Charles. You must convey my regards to Mr. Bennet and his family."

He accepted my decision with a nod, though I could see the eagerness in his eyes was undiminished. "Very well, but you miss an opportunity, I fear. I am told the Bennet daughters are quite the most delightful young ladies in the neighbourhood," he said with a wink before setting off.

Upon his return, I was met with a Charles somewhat deflated in spirit—an uncommon state for a man of his usual vivacity. "Well?" I inquired, curious as to the cause of his discomfiture.

Charles sighed, taking a seat opposite me as he removed his gloves with a touch more force than necessary. "It seems I was doomed to disappointment, Darcy. The ladies of Longbourn were not at home, and so I was denied the pleasure of their company."

I could not help but raise a brow at this. "Surely such a triviality is not cause for such chagrin?"

He shook his head, a rueful smile touching his lips. "Perhaps not, but I had hoped to make their acquaintance. You understand, I have heard much praise of Miss Jane Bennet's beauty, and her sisters are said to be equally accomplished."

I regarded him for a moment, weighing my words. "There will be other opportunities, Charles. The assembly is not far off, and no doubt you will meet the Bennet ladies there."

His mood lifted at this, the shadow of his earlier disappointment chased away by the prospect of the imminent social occasion. "You are right, of course, Darcy. The assembly! That shall be the moment for introductions. And you must promise to attend as well."

I conceded to his request, though the thought of an evening spent in the intricate dance of country society did little to stir my spirits. "I shall attend, though you know well my feelings on such affairs."

Charles laughed, his good humour restored. "Yes, yes, but who knows? You may find yourself surprised by the charms of Hertfordshire's daughters."

I allowed myself a small smile at his teasing, though inwardly I doubted the likelihood of such an occurrence. Nonetheless, I resolved to support Charles in his social endeavours, even if it meant stepping beyond the confines of my own preferences.

As I retire for the evening, I reflect upon the day's events, or rather, the lack thereof. The anticipation of meeting the Bennet family remains unfulfilled, a narrative pause that piques my curiosity despite my usual reserve. It is a curiosity born not of a desire for company, but rather an interest in the characters that inhabit Charles's newfound world—a world that I, by virtue of friendship and circumstance, find myself increasingly drawn into.

Fitzwilliam Darcy

September 1, 1811

In the early morn, as dawn cast its first rays across the dew-laden fields of Netherfield, I found myself preparing for a journey that would once again draw me away from the solace of my own company. Charles, with characteristic ardor, had proposed a sojourn to London to retrieve his sisters, Miss Caroline Bingley and Mrs. Louisa Hurst, along with her husband. These siblings of his hold considerable sway over my friend's disposition, and it is in my interest to maintain cordial relations with them.

The final days of August have come to a close, and with them, a brief reprieve from country life.

On the eve of our departure, Charles's spirits were buoyant with the prospect of reuniting with his family. "Darcy, you must admit there is a certain comfort in the company of one's kin," he said as we dined.

"Indeed," I replied, "though comfort is often accompanied by its own set of expectations and obligations."

He laughed heartily at that. "Ever the philosopher! Come, let us not dwell on the morrow's burdens but rather anticipate the pleasure of familial reunion."

Our journey to London was uneventful, the rhythmic cadence of the carriage wheels a familiar refrain as we traversed the miles separating Netherfield from the city.

Upon our arrival in the city, the cacophony of urban life greeted us with its unrelenting vigor. The townhouse of the Bingleys in Grosvenor Street was as opulent as I remembered, and we were received with all the decorum their station commanded. Caroline's eyes lit up with pleasure upon seeing us, her countenance reflecting the anticipation of the country delights to come. Louisa, ever the more composed of the two, offered a more subdued welcome, her husband, Mr. Hurst, trailing behind with a disinterested air, offered a nod of acknowledgment before resuming his perusal of the morning paper.

"Charles, dear brother, we are quite overcome with excitement at the prospect of Netherfield," Caroline exclaimed, her eyes alight with a blend of anticipation and calculation.

"Indeed," Louisa added, her tone more measured, "we are most eager to see what improvements you have made to the estate."

Charles, ever the gracious host, assured them of Netherfield's readiness to receive them. "You shall find it most agreeable, I am certain. And the neighbourhood is lively with anticipation for the upcoming assembly."

The discussion over dinner turned inevitably to the assembly, and Caroline expressed her intent to outshine the country debutantes with her sophisticated charm and fashion. Her vanity, though thinly veiled, is a trait I have come to expect from her. I offered my own insights on the subject of country assemblies with a reticence that went largely unnoticed amidst the fervor of their planning.

As our stay in London drew to a close, we busied ourselves with the necessary errands and engagements. I called upon my solicitor to discuss several matters pertaining to Pemberley, ensuring that the estate continued to run smoothly in my absence.

The return journey to Netherfield the following day was made in a carriage filled with the Bingleys' luggage and expectations. Caroline's voice, shrill with excitement, dominated the conversation, her every sentence laced with an unspoken competition against the unseen ladies of Hertfordshire. Louisa, more reserved but no less determined, shared her sister's ambition to be admired and courted by the local gentry.

As we set off, Caroline turned to me, a mischievous glint in her eye. "Mr. Darcy, I trust you have prepared yourself for the onslaught of country manners and matchmaking mamas?"

I met her gaze with a wry smile. "Miss Bingley, I assure you that I am fully apprised of the trials that await us. But let us not underestimate the charms of country society too hastily."

She laughed, a sound that did not quite reach her eyes. "Oh, Mr. Darcy, your stoicism is as unassailable as ever."

As the English countryside unfolded before us once more, I found myself contemplating the weeks ahead. The simplicity of country life, which I had hoped to enjoy, now seemed overshadowed by the social ambitions of the Bingley sisters. Their presence at Netherfield, while ensuring Charles' happiness, promised a series of engagements for which I had little appetite.

The rest of the journey back to Netherfield was filled with Caroline's and Louisa's conjectures about the forthcoming assembly, their voices a constant hum of expectation and planning. Mr. Hurst, for his part, seemed content to indulge in the comforts of the carriage and the contents of his flask.

As I pen this entry, the silhouettes of Netherfield's trees are visible against the dusky sky, heralding our return to the estate. Charles's family, with their own distinct personalities and aspirations, will no doubt add a new dimension to our experience of Hertfordshire.

In the silent hours of the evening, I find myself reflecting upon the days ahead. The assembly, with its promise of revelry and socialization, looms large in my thoughts. It is an event that I anticipate with a measure of reservation, yet I cannot deny a certain curiosity regarding the local society and the individuals who comprise it.

For now, I remain a man caught between two worlds—the tranquility of Pemberley and the vitality of Netherfield. Each offers its own lessons and opportunities, and I am resolved to navigate them with the grace and discretion that my position demands.

Fitzwilliam Darcy

September 26, 1811

The night of the Meryton assembly is upon us—a gathering that has been the subject of much anticipation and, I must confess, a significant amount of my own reticence. As I make this entry, the echoes of laughter and music still resonate in my ears, a stark contrast to the silence that now surrounds me in my chambers.

The Meryton assembly—an event which, despite my own reservations, I attended at the insistence of Bingley. His enthusiasm for such occasions is, I must admit, contagious, though it does little to alter my own temperament towards them. In his words, it was to be a night of mirth and merriment, a chance to immerse ourselves in the local society. Yet, as I reflect upon the events of the evening, I find my sentiments decidedly mixed.

Upon our entrance, Bingley was immediately the focus of warm regards and genial welcomes. His amiable and unreserved nature endears him to all, and tonight was no exception. "Darcy," he said, his eyes alight with excitement, "is this not splendid? Such liveliness, such spirit!"

I could only offer a half-smile in response. "Indeed, Bingley, the company seems most... animated."

Charles, true to his nature, was the embodiment of amiability throughout the evening. His countenance, ever agreeable, and his manners, unaffected by the vanity that often plagues men of our standing, drew the admiration of many. It is no surprise that he found himself the object of considerable attention, his lively demeanor endearing him to the company. His sisters, Miss Bingley and Mrs. Hurst, carried themselves with the air of decided fashion that is their trademark, their presence commanding the room as they so deftly do.

Mr. Hurst, though less remarkable in his demeanor, conducted himself with the propriety expected of a gentleman of his standing.

I, however, seemed to have drawn the attention of the room not by any action of my own but by the mere fact of my estate and the fortune it entails. It is an aspect of my life I have come to accept, though it offers little in the way of genuine satisfaction. I was met with a curious mixture of admiration and scrutiny—the former due to the report of my income, which seemed to circulate with preternatural speed, and the latter borne of my own demeanor, which I am told can seem proud and aloof.

The gentlemen present pronounced their approval of my appearance, a sentiment echoed by the ladies, who deemed me handsomer than Bingley—a flattering yet ultimately superficial accolade. For half the evening, I was looked upon with great admiration, but as the night progressed, my reticence to engage in the revelry painted me in a less favourable light.

Bingley, ever the social butterfly, acquainted himself with all the principal people in the room. He danced every dance with a zeal that was commendable, lamenting only that the ball closed too early and speaking of hosting one himself at Netherfield. His amiable qualities spoke for themselves, and the contrast between us was not lost on the assembly.

I danced but twice—once with Mrs. Hurst and once with Miss Bingley, both obligatory gestures of politeness.

Charles, in his characteristic concern for my enjoyment, implored me to join in the dancing. His entreaties, though well-meaning, failed to sway me. The truth of the matter is that I find little enjoyment in a dance with a partner to whom I am not well-acquainted, and the thought of engaging with a lady for no other reason than the expectation of society is one I find insupportable.

It was during this conversation with Charles that I committed an error in judgment—one that, in hindsight, I deeply regret.

"Come, Darcy," he implored, "I must have you dance. I hate to see you standing about by yourself in this stupid manner. You had much better dance."

"I certainly shall not," I replied, my gaze sweeping over the crowd. "You know how I detest it, unless I am particularly acquainted with my partner. At such an assembly as this, it would be insupportable. Your sisters are engaged, and there is not another woman in the room whom it would not be a punishment to me to stand up with."

Bingley, undeterred, pressed on. "I would not be so fastidious as you are," he cried, "for a kingdom! Upon my honour, I never met with so many pleasant girls in my life as I have this evening; and there are several of them, you see, uncommonly pretty."

"You are dancing with the only handsome girl in the room," I said, my attention briefly caught by the eldest Miss Bennet, who possessed a beauty that was acknowledged by all.

"Oh, she is the most beautiful creature I ever beheld! But there is one of her sisters sitting down just behind you, who is very pretty, and I dare say very agreeable. Do let me ask my partner to introduce you."

Upon his insistent, I glanced at Miss Elizabeth Bennet. My words, though whispered in confidence to a friend, were callous and ungentlemanly.—though I knew not her name at the time—she had an air of spirited intelligence, but in that moment, goaded by Bingley's persistence and my own reluctance, I responded poorly. "She is tolerable, but not handsome enough to tempt me; and I am in no humour at present to give consequence to young ladies who are slighted by other men. You had better return to your partner and enjoy her smiles, for you are wasting your time with me."

Bingley, heeding my words, returned to the dance, and I, with a sense of regret for my churlishness, withdrew to a quiet corner of the room. The rest of the evening was spent in observation rather than participation, my character thus decided by the assembly as haughty and unapproachable.

Yet, despite the evening's unfortunate turn, the Bennet family found reasons to rejoice. Mrs. Bennet watched with pride as her eldest daughter, Miss Jane Bennet, received the attentions of Charles and his sisters. The other Bennet sisters, too, found the evening to their satisfaction, with partners aplenty and the merriment that youth and vitality bring.

As for myself, I am left to reflect upon the events of the evening with a sense of disquiet. My pride, a constant companion, has once again proven to be a barrier between myself and the world. The assembly, meant to be an occasion of enjoyment, served as a reminder of the walls I have built around myself—walls that now seem more like a prison than protection.

It was only upon our return to Netherfield that I learned from Bingley the true extent of my folly. Miss Elizabeth had overheard my remarks and shared them with her friends. Her lively disposition found a source of mirth in my unintended slight, and I was left to ponder the repercussions of my pride.

Now, in the solitude of my chamber, I commit these thoughts to paper—a record of an evening fraught with social missteps and the humbling realization that I am perhaps not the man I aspire to be. The journey ahead, both literal and metaphorical, promises to be one of reflection and, I can only hope, personal growth.

Fitzwilliam Darcy

October 12, 1811

It has been some time since I have turned to these pages to unburden my thoughts. Tonight, as the embers in the hearth wane to a soft glow, I find myself compelled to reflect upon the nature of inheritance, friendship, and the differing dispositions that color our interactions with the world.

Charles's acquisition of Netherfield, though born from the unfortunate passing of his father, has brought to light the varied expectations placed upon a man of his means. Nearly a hundred thousand pounds—a fortune that his father intended for the purchase of an estate—now rests in Charles's hands. His father's dreams unfulfilled, the charge to establish the Bingley name within the landed gentry falls to him.

The relative ease and contentment with which Charles has settled into the role of Netherfield's master has not gone unnoticed by his acquaintances. Some speculate whether his temper, so agreeable and unassuming, might lead him to remain here, content as a tenant, and leave the burden of establishing a more permanent seat to his progeny.

His sisters, Caroline and Louisa, harbour their own designs with regards to his fortune. They are keenly aware of the prestige that an estate would confer upon their brother—and by extension, themselves. Caroline, with her sharp wit and discerning eye, presides over his table with an air of entitlement, while Louisa, having secured a match of fashion rather than wealth, sees Netherfield as a sanctuary that suits her when it pleases.

Charles's decision to take Netherfield was made with characteristic impulsiveness. A mere half-hour's consideration was all it took for him to be swayed by the estate's situation and the owner's assurances. His temperament, so readily open to suggestion and so devoid of artifice, stands in stark contrast to my own.

Our friendship, steadfast as it is, often gives me pause to consider how such opposites in character have come to form so close a bond. Where Charles is all ease and openness, I am often perceived as haughty and reserved. My manners, though I strive for civility, lack the inviting warmth that comes so naturally to him. It is a truth I cannot deny, nor can I dismiss the notion that my comportment has, at times, caused offence where none was intended.

The recent Meryton assembly serves as a fitting illustration of this dichotomy between us. Charles speaks of the event with unbridled enthusiasm, praising the amiable nature of the attendees and extolling the beauty of the Bennet sisters—Miss Jane Bennet, in particular, whom he regards as an angelic vision.

I, however, recall the evening with a far more critical eye. The company struck me as lacking in both beauty and fashion, and I found little interest or pleasure in the gathering. My admission of Miss Bennet's attractiveness was tempered by the observation that she smiled more than I deemed proper—a comment that, I have since learned, did not escape the notice of Caroline and Louisa, who nevertheless found her to be a sweet girl worthy of their brother's attention.

It is in moments such as these that I am reminded of the weight of my own judgments and the influence they may hold over Charles.

His reliance on my regard and opinion is a responsibility I do not take lightly. Yet, I must also acknowledge that in matters of understanding, my perception may be clouded by a disposition that is at times overly fastidious.

As I close this entry, I am left to consider the path that lies before us. Netherfield, for the present, is Charles's domain, and he is well-liked by all who cross its threshold. For myself, I must strive to temper my own nature with a more generous spirit, lest I continue to give offence and alienate those who might otherwise become companions, or perhaps more.

In the silence of my chamber, I ponder these thoughts, recognizing that the journey ahead is not merely one of miles and estates, but also of self-examination and, perhaps, change.

Fitzwilliam Darcy

October 17, 1811

As the autumn leaves begin their descent, tracing lazy spirals to the ground, today's entry is one of secondhand accounts and the musings they provoke. It was Caroline Bingley and her sister Mrs. Hurst who ventured forth to return the social visit to the Bennets of Longbourn, whilst I remained at Netherfield, occupied with estate correspondence that demanded my attention.

Upon their return, the drawing room at Netherfield was set alight with their impressions and judgments, delivered with the fervency that only fresh gossip can inspire. It was through their lively discussion that I gleaned insight into the character and atmosphere of Longbourn.

Caroline was the first to offer her observations, her tone laced with a condescension that she scarcely bothered to veil. "The two elder Miss Bennets are indeed a credit to their family," she began, folding her hands neatly in her lap. "Miss Jane Bennet, in particular, is a vision of demure beauty; she has a sweetness of character that one cannot help but admire."

Mrs. Hurst, reclining on a chaise with a posture that spoke of refined indolence, chimed in with a nod of agreement. "True, the mother is quite beyond the pale—vulgar and matchmaking. And as for the younger sisters, they are simply not worth mentioning. But Jane and Elizabeth Bennet have a certain quality that sets them apart."

I listened intently, though I offered no interjection. The mention of Elizabeth caught my attention, her image coming to mind unbidden—a testament to the impression she had made upon me, however reluctantly admitted.

Caroline continued, "Elizabeth Bennet has an ease about her, a quickness of mind that is... rather singular. She is not as handsome as her sister, but there is a playfulness in her manner that is quite endearing."

Her words echoed the thoughts I myself had harbored since our initial encounter at the Meryton assembly, though I had yet to voice them so candidly.

Charles, ever the optimist, was buoyed by their report. "I am pleased to hear that my high opinion of the Miss Bennets is shared by others. Jane is an angel, and Elizabeth—well, she is quite remarkable in her own right."

The visit, while performed out of social duty, had offered a glimpse into the dynamics of the Bennet household—a household that, despite its varied characters, had managed to capture the interest of Netherfield's occupants in unexpected ways.

The conversation drifted then to other matters, but my mind lingered on the Bennet sisters and the varying perceptions they evoked. It was clear that Charles's admiration for Jane was deepening with each encounter, and even Caroline and Louisa, despite their initial reservations, had found qualities to praise in the elder Bennets.

Retiring to my study later in the evening, I found myself ruminating on the complexities of social hierarchy and the ease with which the Bingley sisters dismissed those whom they deemed inferior.

Yet, in the midst of such dismissal, the Bennet sisters had emerged with a measure of esteem—a testament to their own merits.

The web of relationships forming around us is intricate and, at times, unpredictable. I find myself drawn into its pattern, intrigued by the interactions and the subtle dance of society. The Bennets, particularly Elizabeth, with her lively eyes and unguarded expressions, present a puzzle that both challenges and compels me.

As the night deepens and the candlelight wanes, I commit these reflections to paper—a silent observer piecing together the tableau of Hertfordshire life from the narratives presented to me. What role I shall play in this unfolding drama remains to be seen, but it is becoming increasingly evident that my journey here will not be one of mere spectatorship.

Fitzwilliam Darcy

November 5, 1811

The social wheel continues to turn here in Hertfordshire, and I find myself once again a participant in its rounds. This evening, we were amongst the guests at Sir William Lucas's—a gathering characterized by the usual conviviality of such affairs, and yet not without its revelations.

The conversation that has given rise to much contemplation this night was not one in which I partook, but rather one I observed from a close distance. It was a discourse between Miss Elizabeth Bennet and her friend, Miss Charlotte Lucas, concerning the nature of affection and the stratagems of courtship.

Miss Lucas, whose pragmatism borders on the cynical, advocated for a more active role on the part of women in securing an attachment, citing the necessity of encouragement in the face of male reticence. Miss Bennet's rebuttal was spirited, as I have come to expect, insisting that her sister's genuine and uncontrived behavior towards Mr. Bingley should be sufficient to elicit his admiration, without resort to artifice.

Their exchange lingered with me, for it brought into sharp relief the delicate balance between sincerity and strategy in matters of the heart—a balance I have long observed, but seldom engaged with.

As the evening progressed, I found myself, not for the first time, drawn to Miss Elizabeth Bennet's conversation. There is an ease about her, a liveliness that seems to challenge the solemnity of my own character. Her words to Colonel Forster were delivered with such animation that I could not help but overhear, and though I had resolved to maintain a distance, I found myself drawn into their orbit.

When Miss Lucas inquired as to my attentiveness, Miss Elizabeth responded with a playfulness that bordered on impertinence—a quality that, rather than repelling me, piqued my curiosity further.

"Did not you think, Mr. Darcy, that I expressed myself uncommonly well just now, when I was teasing Colonel Forster to give us a ball at Meryton?" she inquired, her eyes alight with mischief.

"With great energy," I replied, striving to match her tone. "But it is a subject which always makes a lady energetic."

"You are severe on us," she countered.

I was about to offer a rejoinder when Sir William Lucas approached, intent on performing the role of affable host. His insistence on the merits of dancing, and his pointed suggestion that I should partner with Miss Elizabeth, led to a curious interlude wherein she refused my belated offer with a mix of mirth and decisiveness that left me at once bemused and impressed.

"Indeed, sir, I have not the least intention of dancing. I entreat you not to suppose that I moved this way in order to beg for a partner."

The remainder of the evening saw Miss Elizabeth and her sister perform musically for the company. While I have no particular expertise in the art, it was evident to any observer that Miss Elizabeth's talents, though modest, were delivered with a grace and ease sadly lacking in her sister Mary's more studied performance.

Caroline Bingley's approach interrupted my observations, her voice tinged with the forced cheer of one who seeks to draw attention to herself. "I can guess the subject of your reverie," she declared, an expectant look upon her face.

"You are mistaken," I assured her, and yet, as the conversation progressed, I found myself admitting to a newfound appreciation for the effect of fine eyes—specifically, those belonging to Miss Elizabeth Bennet. Caroline's reaction was one of astonishment and thinly veiled displeasure, a testament to the rivalry she perceives between herself and the younger Bennet.

"Miss Elizabeth Bennet!" repeated Miss Bingley. I am all astonishment. How long has she been such a favourite? and pray when am I to wish you joy?"

"That is exactly the question which I expected you to ask. A lady's imagination is very rapid; it jumps from admiration to love, from love to matrimony, in a moment. I knew you would be wishing me joy."

"Nay, if you are so serious about it, I shall consider the matter as absolutely settled. You will have a charming mother-in-law, indeed, and of course she will be always at Pemberley with you."

Caroline, ever quick to seize upon the undercurrents of social discourse, questioned the sudden favor in which I held Miss Elizabeth, her words dripping with incredulity and a touch of malice. Her jest that I was soon to be ensnared in matrimony was met with the indifference it deserved, yet it served to underscore the shifting sands beneath my feet—the nascent realization that my interest in Elizabeth Bennet was growing deeper than mere amusement.

I pondered this as I watched the younger guests dance with abandon, their laughter echoing in the chamber. The moment was pierced by Sir William Lucas's approach, his conversation as predictably focused on the merits of dancing as ever. His efforts to compliment Bingley and myself on our supposed skill were met with a civility born of obligation rather than agreement.

The night's exchanges continued to weigh heavily upon me as I retired to my chambers. Elizabeth Bennet's playful defiance, her refusal to dance, her readiness to challenge my perceptions—these were not the actions of a woman seeking to ingratiate herself or to secure a prosperous match. They were the actions of someone with a mind and will of her own, a refreshing departure from the calculated maneuvers so often at play in the circles I usually frequent.

What is it about her that so intrigues me? Is it the very challenge she presents to my understanding of the world and my place within it? Or is there something more, a depth of character I yearn to comprehend, a spirit that calls to something long dormant within me?

These questions linger as I pen this entry. The image of Elizabeth, her head thrown back in laughter, her eyes sparkling with intelligence and wit, has imprinted itself upon my memory. I am a man accustomed to control, to the careful management of my affairs and my emotions. Yet, as I concede to the silence of the night, I must acknowledge a certain disquiet, an awareness that my interest in Miss Elizabeth Bennet may herald the beginning of a journey for which I am wholly unprepared.

The tapestry of life at Netherfield is becoming more complex, threaded with new colors and patterns that disrupt the familiar weave. As I close this journal, I am left to wonder at the role Elizabeth Bennet will play in the unfolding narrative, and at the transformation that may be required of me to truly understand her.

Fitzwilliam Darcy

November 5, 1811

The social wheel continues to turn here in Hertfordshire, and I find myself once again a participant in its rounds. This evening, we were amongst the guests at Sir William Lucas's—a gathering characterized by the usual conviviality of such affairs, and yet not without its revelations.

The conversation that has given rise to much contemplation this night was not one in which I partook, but rather one I observed from a close distance. It was a discourse between Miss Elizabeth Bennet and her friend, Miss Charlotte Lucas, concerning the nature of affection and the stratagems of courtship.

Miss Lucas, whose pragmatism borders on the cynical, advocated for a more active role on the part of women in securing an attachment, citing the necessity of encouragement in the face of male reticence. Miss Bennet's rebuttal was spirited, as I have come to expect, insisting that her sister's genuine and uncontrived behavior towards Mr. Bingley should be sufficient to elicit his admiration, without resort to artifice.

Their exchange lingered with me, for it brought into sharp relief the delicate balance between sincerity and strategy in matters of the heart—a balance I have long observed, but seldom engaged with.

As the evening progressed, I found myself, not for the first time, drawn to Miss Elizabeth Bennet's conversation. There is an ease about her, a liveliness that seems to challenge the solemnity of my own character. Her words to Colonel Forster were delivered with such animation that I could not help but overhear, and though I had resolved to maintain a distance, I found myself drawn into their orbit.

When Miss Lucas inquired as to my attentiveness, Miss Elizabeth responded with a playfulness that bordered on impertinence—a quality that, rather than repelling me, piqued my curiosity further.

"Did not you think, Mr. Darcy, that I expressed myself uncommonly well just now, when I was teasing Colonel Forster to give us a ball at Meryton?" she inquired, her eyes alight with mischief.

"With great energy," I replied, striving to match her tone. "But it is a subject which always makes a lady energetic."

"You are severe on us," she countered.

I was about to offer a rejoinder when Sir William Lucas approached, intent on performing the role of affable host. His insistence on the merits of dancing, and his pointed suggestion that I should partner with Miss Elizabeth, led to a curious interlude wherein she refused my belated offer with a mix of mirth and decisiveness that left me at once bemused and impressed.

"Indeed, sir, I have not the least intention of dancing. I entreat you not to suppose that I moved this way in order to beg for a partner."

The remainder of the evening saw Miss Elizabeth and her sister perform musically for the company. While I have no particular expertise in the art, it was evident to any observer that Miss Elizabeth's talents, though modest, were delivered with a grace and ease sadly lacking in her sister Mary's more studied performance.

Caroline Bingley's approach interrupted my observations, her voice tinged with the forced cheer of one who seeks to draw attention to herself. "I can guess the subject of your reverie," she declared, an expectant look upon her face.

"You are mistaken," I assured her, and yet, as the conversation progressed, I found myself admitting to a newfound appreciation for the effect of fine eyes—specifically, those belonging to Miss Elizabeth Bennet. Caroline's reaction was one of astonishment and thinly veiled displeasure, a testament to the rivalry she perceives between herself and the younger Bennet.

"Miss Elizabeth Bennet!" repeated Miss Bingley. I am all astonishment. How long has she been such a favourite? and pray when am I to wish you joy?"

"That is exactly the question which I expected you to ask. A lady's imagination is very rapid; it jumps from admiration to love, from love to matrimony, in a moment. I knew you would be wishing me joy."

"Nay, if you are so serious about it, I shall consider the matter as absolutely settled. You will have a charming mother-in-law, indeed, and of course she will be always at Pemberley with you."

Caroline, ever quick to seize upon the undercurrents of social discourse, questioned the sudden favor in which I held Miss Elizabeth, her words dripping with incredulity and a touch of malice. Her jest that

I was soon to be ensnared in matrimony was met with the indifference it deserved, yet it served to underscore the shifting sands beneath my feet—the nascent realization that my interest in Elizabeth Bennet was growing deeper than mere amusement.

I pondered this as I watched the younger guests dance with abandon, their laughter echoing in the chamber. The moment was pierced by Sir William Lucas's approach, his conversation as predictably focused on the merits of dancing as ever. His efforts to compliment Bingley and myself on our supposed skill were met with a civility born of obligation rather than agreement.

The night's exchanges continued to weigh heavily upon me as I retired to my chambers. Elizabeth Bennet's playful defiance, her refusal to dance, her readiness to challenge my perceptions—these were not the actions of a woman seeking to ingratiate herself or to secure a prosperous match. They were the actions of someone with a mind and will of her own, a refreshing departure from the calculated maneuvers so often at play in the circles I usually frequent.

What is it about her that so intrigues me? Is it the very challenge she presents to my understanding of the world and my place within it? Or is there something more, a depth of character I yearn to comprehend, a spirit that calls to something long dormant within me?

These questions linger as I pen this entry. The image of Elizabeth, her head thrown back in laughter, her eyes sparkling with intelligence and wit, has imprinted itself upon my memory. I am a man accustomed to control, to the careful management of my affairs and my emotions. Yet, as I concede to the silence of the night, I must acknowledge a certain disquiet, an awareness that my interest in Miss Elizabeth Bennet may herald the beginning of a journey for which I am wholly unprepared.

The tapestry of life at Netherfield is becoming more complex, threaded with new colors and patterns that disrupt the familiar weave. As I close this journal, I am left to wonder at the role Elizabeth Bennet will play in the unfolding narrative, and at the transformation that may be required of me to truly understand her.

Fitzwilliam Darcy

November 15, 1811

This morning's atmosphere at Netherfield was disrupted by a simple yet consequential act—the dispatch of a note by Miss Bingley to Miss Jane Bennet. It was a seemingly innocuous invitation to dine, devoid of the grandeur of balls or the solemnity of formal receptions. Yet, as the hours unfolded, it became a fulcrum upon which the day's events would pivot.

I learned of this development not firsthand, but through the recounting of others. Miss Bingley, returning from dispatching her servant, was all self-satisfaction as she regaled us with the particulars of her missive. "I have sent an invitation to dear Jane Bennet for this afternoon," she announced with a flourish. "A little feminine society shall be just the thing to brighten this dreary day."

I must confess to a measure of indifference at the time, my thoughts occupied with matters of estate and the letters from Pemberley that demanded my attention. Little did I realize the chain of events that Miss Bingley's invitation would set in motion.

It was late afternoon when word reached Netherfield of Miss Bennet's arrival—not in the comfort of a carriage, as decorum would dictate, but rather drenched from a journey made on horseback under skies that had opened with relentless rain. The folly of such a choice was apparent to all, and I could not suppress a furrow of concern upon my brow. To venture out in such weather was to invite ill health, and for what purpose? To satisfy the whims of social engagement?

The manner in which Miss Bennet's arrival was received varied greatly within our party. Miss Bingley and Mrs. Hurst fluttered about with exclamations of dismay and thinly veiled delight at the dramatic turn of events. Charles, bless his soul, was the epitome of concern, rushing to offer every comfort and assistance to Miss Bennet. As for myself, I stood somewhat apart, observing the scene with a growing sense of disquiet.

The hours that followed were marked by a tension that hung heavy in the air. Miss Bennet, it transpired, had taken ill—a predictable outcome, given the circumstances of her journey. Charles's distress was palpable, and I found myself sharing in his concern, albeit with a more reserved expression. The recklessness of the decision to ride in such weather, the apparent disregard for her own well-being—these thoughts circled in my mind, coupled with the recognition that the one who had most to lose from this turn of events was now confined to a guest chamber, battling the effects of her exposure to the elements.

Dinner that evening was a subdued affair, the empty seat at the table a reminder of the reason for our concern. Miss Bingley, ever the hostess, attempted to maintain a semblance of normalcy, but her efforts were belied by the occasional glance towards the staircase, as if expecting news to descend at any moment.

As the night drew on, I retired to the solitude of the library, the quiet a stark contrast to the flurry of activity that had characterized the day. It was there, amidst the leather-bound tomes and the flickering light of the hearth, that I allowed myself a rare moment of introspection.

The image of Elizabeth Bennet, fraught with worry for her sister, came unbidden to my mind. Her strength of character, her fierce loyalty—these were qualities that commanded my respect. And yet, they also gave rise to a dissonance within me—a conflict between my inclination to maintain a certain detachment and the impulse to offer comfort, to extend the hand of friendship in a time of need.

As I pen this entry, the rain continues its relentless assault upon the windowpanes, each droplet a reminder of the day's events. The situation in which we find ourselves is a testament to the unpredictable nature of life, to the unforeseen consequences that can arise from the most mundane of decisions.

Miss Bennet's health, and the effect her condition may have on those around her, weighs heavily on my mind as I close this journal. The morrow is uncertain, and I find myself more invested in the outcome than I would have previously cared to admit.

Fitzwilliam Darcy

November 16, 1811

The morning broke with a pall of clouds that seemed to presage the tumult of emotions that would unfold throughout the day. As I sat in the solitude of my study, a knock at the door announced the arrival of a visitor whose appearance would set the tone for the remainder of our time at Netherfield.

The early hours of this morning were marked by a decision most extraordinary, demonstrating the force of character that resides within Miss Elizabeth Bennet. Upon learning of her sister's indisposition, she resolved to traverse the muddy fields between Longbourn and Netherfield on foot—an undertaking that, while it showcased her determination and affection, also raised questions of propriety and decorum.

"Mr. Darcy, Miss Elizabeth Bennet has arrived on foot to attend to her sister," I was informed by an astonished member of the staff. The image of her braving the three-mile walk from Longbourn through muddy fields and inclement weather filled me with a mixture of disbelief and reluctant admiration.

The breakfast room was a scene of commotion as she entered, her countenance flushed with exertion, her apparel marked by the journey. Her appearance was met with a mix of reactions, each betraying the character of the observer.

Miss Bingley was quick to voice her surprise, thinly veiled as concern, "Miss Bennet, to walk in such weather! And by yourself! It is most improper."

Elizabeth's response was immediate and composed, betraying no offense at the insinuation of impropriety. "I am quite fit to see my sister, which is all I wish," she replied, her eyes betraying none of the turmoil that her bold action must have incited within.

Bingley, ever the gentleman, offered his sympathies with genuine warmth, "Miss Elizabeth, I am most earnestly sorry for your discomfort. Pray, let us attend to you."

I, however, remained silent, my thoughts ensnared by the complexity of my feelings. Her resolve was commendable, yet it defied the conventions of society. It was a testament to her devotion—an attribute I found myself increasingly drawn to, despite my better judgment.

It was during dinner that Elizabeth's absence allowed for unguarded conversation. Miss Bingley seized the opportunity to disparage her further. "Her manners were pronounced to be very bad indeed, a mixture of pride and impertinence; she had no conversation, no style, no taste, no beauty," she declared with a scoff.

Mrs. Hurst was quick to agree, "I could hardly keep my countenance. Very nonsensical to come at all! Why must she be scampering about the country because her sister had a cold?"

I found myself unable to partake in their derision, my esteem for Elizabeth's character growing with each unwarranted critique. Bingley, too, was unwilling to concede to his sisters' censure. "I thought Miss Elizabeth Bennet looked remarkably well when she came into the room this morning. Her dirty petticoat quite escaped my notice," he said, a testament to his unaffected regard for her.

"You observed it, Mr. Darcy, I am sure," Miss Bingley pressed, expecting me to concur with their ridicule. Yet, I could not.

The conversation shifted then to the Bennet's connections in trade, a subject that provided much amusement for the Bingley sisters. "I think I have heard you say that their uncle is an attorney in Meryton?" I inquired, more to draw out their prejudices than out of any real interest.

"Yes; and they have another, who lives somewhere near Cheapside," Miss Bingley replied, her laughter ringing with scorn.

"That is capital," Mrs. Hurst added, joining in her sister's merriment.

Bingley, however, would not be swayed by their shallow judgments. "If they had uncles enough to fill all Cheapside, it would not make them one jot less agreeable," he retorted.

"But it must very materially lessen their chance of marrying men of any consideration in the world," I found myself saying, echoing the sentiment of the time, yet feeling a twinge of regret at the words even as they left my lips.

It was after dinner that the true nature of the Bingley sisters' character was revealed. In the absence of Elizabeth, they took to speaking of her with a scorn that I found distasteful. Her lack of style, her impertinence, her audacity to brave the mud and rain—all were subjects of their ridicule. I could not join in their mirth, and Mr. Bingley's defense of Elizabeth's fine eyes, though it was meant to be humorous, struck a chord within me that resonated with a truth I was only beginning to acknowledge.

The evening progressed with Jane's health at the forefront of our attentions. Elizabeth was steadfast by her sister's side, a sentinel of familial duty. The hours she spent in Jane's company spoke volumes of the depth of their sisterly bond, leaving the rest of us to navigate the awkwardness of her unexpected residence among us.

Elizabeth's presence at Netherfield became an established fact, her extended stay necessitated by her sister's illness and the inclement weather. The offer of the carriage for her return was extended and then retracted as Jane's condition warranted her sister's constant care. Thus, arrangements were made to accommodate Elizabeth's unintended residency, a matter that seemed to please Mr. Bingley greatly and cause no small amount of consternation to his sisters.

As the night deepened and I retired to reflect upon the day's events, it was with a growing awareness that Elizabeth Bennet, with her unabashed sincerity and disregard for societal judgment, was drawing forth from me a mixture of respect and fascination. Her influence, though subtle, was beginning to challenge my own long-held beliefs about status, propriety, and the nature of true gentility.

In the privacy of these pages, I confess that my thoughts are increasingly occupied by Elizabeth. Her vitality, her loyalty, her unguarded moments of vulnerability—these are qualities that stir something within me, prompting both introspection and a desire to know more of her inner world.

Fitzwilliam Darcy

November 19, 1811

As the hours of the day waned, a curious repartee unfolded in the drawing room of Netherfield. It was a scene punctuated by the wit and intellect of those present, and yet, it was underscored by an undercurrent of tension and rivalry, the cause of which I was becoming increasingly conscious.

Miss Bingley, ever poised to assert her presence, engaged me in a dialogue that was as much about displaying her own erudition as it was a challenge to Miss Elizabeth Bennet.

Mr. Hurst interjected, "Do you prefer reading to cards?" said he; "that is rather singular."

Miss Bingley seized the opportunity to paint Elizabeth in a light less flattering, though her words missed their mark.

"Miss Eliza Bennet," said Miss Bingley, "despises cards. She is a great reader, and has no pleasure in anything else."

Elizabeth, who had overheard the exchange, was quick to correct her with a gentle rebuke. "I deserve neither such praise nor such censure," she said. "I am not a great reader, and I have pleasure in many things."

It was Bingley who diffused the moment with a grace befitting his character. "In nursing your sister, I am sure you have pleasure," he said to Elizabeth, "and I hope it will soon be increased by seeing her quite well."

Elizabeth expressed her gratitude with a warmth that seemed to brighten the room, and then she moved towards a table where a few books lay—a modest collection that nevertheless provided a segue for further discussion.

The topic of libraries and literature became the new battleground upon which Miss Bingley sought to distinguish herself, praising the grandeur of Pemberley's collection and lamenting the inadequacy of their own. I affirmed the value of such a collection, alluding to the generations of care that had shaped it, and the personal efforts I had made to enhance its worth.

As the conversation meandered towards the subject of accomplished women, a topic I found myself drawn into with unexpected fervor, I was struck by the divergence between Miss Bingley's understanding of the term and my own. To be truly accomplished, I argued, a woman must possess more than the superficial trappings of the arts. She must have a thorough knowledge of music, singing, drawing, dancing, and the modern languages, as well as a certain something in her air and manner of walking.

Elizabeth's participation in the debate was as insightful as it was provocative. "Then," she observed, "you must comprehend a great deal in your idea of an accomplished woman." Her words challenged us to define our expectations, and in doing so, revealed the narrowness of our assumptions.

The discourse continued, with Mrs. Hurst and Miss Bingley protesting the rarity of such paragons of virtue, until the interjection of Mr. Hurst, whose attention to the card game far exceeded his interest in our philosophical musings, brought it to an abrupt end.

It was not long after that Elizabeth excused herself, her concern for her sister drawing her away from our company. In her absence, Miss Bingley resumed her criticism, this time unencumbered by the object of her disdain. "Eliza Bennet is one of those young ladies who seek to recommend themselves to the other sex by undervaluing their own," she declared, a statement I found to be grossly unfair.

"Whatever bears affinity to cunning is despicable," I found myself agreeing, though my mind was not on the conversation but on Elizabeth's hasty departure. Her devotion to her sister was beyond reproach, a devotion that, I begrudgingly admitted, commanded my admiration.

The evening concluded with the usual diversions—music and light entertainment—but the joy of it was marred by the undercurrent of concern for Miss Bennet's health. Bingley, showing the depth of his character, gave orders to ensure the comfort of the Bennet sisters, a gesture that did not go unnoticed by me.

As I retire to pen these thoughts, I am left to ponder the complexities of the day. The evolving dynamic between Elizabeth and myself, her evident virtues, and the ignoble conduct of those who would belittle her, are matters that weigh heavily upon my mind. In the quiet of the night, I find myself questioning the very foundations of my beliefs and the nature of my regard for Miss Elizabeth Bennet.

Fitzwilliam Darcy

November 20, 1811

An early visitation was made upon us at Netherfield this day, as Mrs. Bennet, along with her two youngest daughters, made their way to inquire after Miss Bennet's health. The anxiety that hung about the mother seemed not entirely for the wellbeing of her daughter, but also for the potential consequences her recovery might imply regarding their stay.

Upon examination, Mr. Jones—the local apothecary—affirmed the severity of Miss Bennet's illness, warranting her continued residence under our roof. Mrs. Bennet's relief at this news was palpable, and she readily accepted Miss Bingley's invitation to join the breakfast parlour. Mr. Bingley met them with his characteristic goodwill, expressing hopes that Mrs. Bennet had not found her daughter's condition to be worse than expected.

"Indeed I have, sir," Mrs. Bennet replied with an air of affected concern. "She is a great deal too ill to be moved. Mr. Jones says we must not think of moving her. We must trespass a little longer on your kindness."

"Removed!" cried Bingley. "It must not be thought of. My sister, I am sure, will not hear of her removal."

"You may depend upon it, madam," said Miss Bingley, with cold civility, "that Miss Bennet shall receive every possible attention while she remains with us."

The conversation that followed was a delicate dance, each participant playing their part with varying degrees of sincerity. Miss Bingley offered assurances of her brother's willingness to host Miss Bennet for as long as necessary, and Mrs. Bennet was profuse in her gratitude, seizing the opportunity to extol the virtues of Netherfield and its master.

Elizabeth's entry into the discussion was marked by her usual poise and perceptiveness, engaging Mr. Bingley in a playful exchange about his ability to remain fixed in his decisions. It was an interaction that I observed closely, for in her words, I discerned a keen understanding of character—a trait that set her apart from others.

"You begin to comprehend me, do you?" Mr. Bingley asked, directing his attention towards Elizabeth.

"Oh yes—I understand you perfectly," she assured him.

The exchange between them allowed me a glimpse into Elizabeth's discerning nature, and her subsequent conversation with her mother further highlighted her efforts to navigate the social complexities of our gathering with grace.

As the morning progressed, the dialogue meandered through topics of character study, the merits of town and country, and the attributes of an accomplished woman—a subject that seemed to capture the interest of all present. It was during this discourse that I found myself unexpectedly aligned with Elizabeth in our understanding of true accomplishment, a sentiment that appeared to surprise even Miss Bingley.

Mrs. Bennet's interjections, though well-intentioned, often bordered on the indelicate, prompting Elizabeth to intervene with subtle redirections. The exchanges, at times, bordered on the contentious, but it was the unaffected civility of Mr. Bingley that maintained a semblance of harmony.

The visit concluded with Mrs. Bennet ordering her carriage, not before Lydia, her youngest, boldly reminded Mr. Bingley of his promise to host a ball—a reminder that elicited from him a commitment that was as generous as it was calculated to please.

"I am perfectly ready, I assure you, to keep my engagement; and, when your sister is recovered, you shall, if you please, name the very day of the ball. But you would not wish to be dancing while she is ill?"

Lydia declared herself satisfied. "Oh yes!

As the Bennet ladies took their leave, I reflected upon the morning's events. The interactions had laid bare the nuances of our social fabric, the threads of which were woven with expectations, propriety, and the unspoken rules that govern our conduct.

In the quiet that followed their departure, I found myself contemplating the peculiarities of Elizabeth Bennet's character. Her intelligence, her wit, and her evident devotion to her family painted a portrait of a woman whose complexity was becoming increasingly endearing to me.

As I retire to my chambers this evening, I do so with a mind preoccupied by the day's conversations and the realization that my interest in Elizabeth Bennet continues to deepen, challenging my notions of what is proper, what is expected, and what is truly worthy of admiration.

Fitzwilliam Darcy

November 21, 1811

The day unfolded with a rhythm now familiar, punctuated by the quiet ticking of the clock and the soft murmurs of concern for the convalescing Miss Bennet. The hours were marked by small events—Mrs. Hurst and Miss Bingley attending to the patient, Mr. Bingley and Mr. Hurst engaging in their card games, and Miss Elizabeth Bennet, with her needlework in hand, observing the social theater that played out before her.

I found myself at the writing desk, penning a letter to my sister, Georgiana, a task that required a level of concentration I struggled to maintain amidst the distractions provided by Miss Bingley. Her attempts to draw me into conversation were relentless, her voice a siren's call demanding attention I was reluctant to give.

"How delighted Miss Darcy will be to receive such a letter!" she exclaimed, her tone a mixture of flattery and intrusion.

I offered no response, my focus unwavering.

"You write uncommonly fast," she continued, undeterred by my silence.

"You are mistaken. I write rather slowly," I corrected her, without lifting my gaze from the parchment.

The interplay continued, Miss Bingley commenting on the business of letter-writing, the quality of my penmanship, and even the content of my correspondence, all the while insinuating herself into my presence with an intimacy that was unearned and, frankly, unwelcome.

Elizabeth, for her part, seemed content to observe our exchange, her expressions betraying an understanding of the dynamics at play. I was acutely aware of her gaze upon us, her attention flitting between her needlework and the dialogue that unfolded.

The conversation soon shifted to the topic of accomplishments and the nature of our society, a discourse that had become a recurring theme in our gatherings. Mr. Bingley's lighthearted remarks about the ubiquity of accomplished young ladies elicited from me a more critical perspective, one that suggested a depth of character and intellect was required to truly merit the title.

Elizabeth's contributions to the conversation were astute, her insights cutting to the heart of the matter, and it was in this exchange that I felt a kinship with her—a shared understanding that transcended the superficialities of our social circle.

Miss Bingley, always eager to exhibit her proficiency, acceded with alacrity and approached the pianoforte with a beaming countenance. Elizabeth, however, demurred, resisting the polite insistence with a modesty that seemed genuine rather than affected.

As Mrs. Hurst joined her sister in harmonious concert, I found myself unable to focus entirely on the performance. My gaze, it seems, was drawn to Elizabeth, who was engaged in perusing the music-books that lay upon the instrument. The peculiarity of her catching my eye so often was not lost on me, and I pondered the reason behind such attention. Was it mere coincidence, or something more deliberate?

Her thoughts on my gaze were unknown to me, though I could hazard a guess that she found it either disconcerting or inconsequential. Elizabeth was not one to be easily discomposed, and the notion that I, of all people, could be an object of her scrutiny was both perplexing and strangely gratifying.

The music continued, Miss Bingley transitioning from Italian melodies to a lively Scotch air, the notes floating through the room like a spirited breeze. It was then that I found occasion to approach Elizabeth, my inquiry about her inclination to dance a reel meant in jest, yet also as an attempt to engage her further.

Her response was not immediate, and when it came, it was laced with an archness that caught me off guard. "I have made up my mind to tell you that I do not want to dance a reel at all; and now despise me if you dare," she challenged.

"Indeed I do not dare," was my reply, an admittance of the truth, for in her presence, I found myself disarmingly captivated.

The interlude was observed by Miss Bingley, whose jealousy was thinly veiled. Her desire for the recovery of her friend Jane was now mingled with a determination to rid herself of Elizabeth—a goal she pursued with a subtlety that was anything but subtle.

Later this evening, as we walked in the shrubbery, Miss Bingley seized the moment to provoke me with talk of the supposed marriage between Elizabeth and myself. Her words were pointed, her suggestions about Elizabeth's family pointedly disparaging. Yet, it was her allusion to Elizabeth's eyes that stayed with me, a begrudging acknowledgment of their beauty that I could not deny.

Our conversation was abruptly interrupted by the arrival of Mrs. Hurst and Elizabeth. Miss Bingley's abrupt departure with Mrs. Hurst, taking my arm and leaving Elizabeth to walk alone, was a maneuver of calculated exclusion. My protest was immediate, calling for a change of path that would accommodate all, but Elizabeth's refusal was swift and delivered with a jest that belied any affront.

As she departed with a laughter in her step, I could not help but admire her resilience and spirit. Her absence left an unexpected void, and as I watched her retreat, I found myself considering the peculiar position I was in—admiring a woman whose connections I could not countenance, yet whose presence I could not seem to disregard.

The remainder of the day passed in contemplation and conversation, the ordinary ebb and flow of country life at Netherfield gently disrupted by the extraordinary influence of Elizabeth Bennet. Her vitality and defiance of convention were as refreshing as they were confounding, challenging my notions of what was desirable and proper.

As I close this entry, I am left to wonder at the path ahead. I am drawn to her, against my better judgment, and find myself in a constant state of anticipation for our next encounter. Elizabeth Bennet has become a puzzle I am intent on solving, even as I suspect that the solution may unsettle the very foundations of my world.

Fitzwilliam Darcy

November 23, 1811

The post-dinner hours unfolded in a manner that has become customary during our residence at Netherfield, yet with each passing day, the familiarity of routine is coupled with a sharpening awareness of the nuances within our company. The presence of Elizabeth Bennet continues to cast a distinctive hue upon these gatherings, her spirit and intelligence an ever-present undercurrent to the evening's repose.

Upon the ladies' retreat from the dining room, I took up residence with a book, seeking the quiet refuge of its pages. Yet, the tranquility I desired was not to be found this night. The drawing room became a stage upon which the subtle interplay of character and desire was silently enacted, and I found myself an unwilling actor in this silent drama.

Elizabeth approached her sister with a tenderness that spoke volumes of her devotion, ensuring her comfort with the solicitousness of a guardian. The warmth exhibited by Bingley towards Jane was equally apparent, a clear indication of his deepening affection, and one that did not escape the notice of those present. His attentions were singular and pointed, and Elizabeth observed the scene with a mixture of satisfaction and amusement.

The proposed card game was dismissed as I was well known to not desire such amusements. Thus, I engaged with a book, seeking to occupy my mind with the written word rather than the complex social dynamics unfolding around me. Yet Miss Bingley, who had taken up a book herself, seemed to find her own text far less absorbing than mine, her eyes and inquiries frequently straying in my direction.

In time, her efforts to draw me out proved futile, and in a moment of exasperation, she exclaimed the virtues of reading as the pinnacle of evening entertainment—a sentiment which, under different circumstances, might have found agreement in me. But the hollow ring of her words did not escape my notice, nor did they inspire a response from the company.

"How pleasant it is to spend an evening in this way!" Miss Bingley eventually declared, her voice tinged with a boredom that belied her words. "I declare after all there is no enjoyment like reading!" The irony of her statement, given her evident restlessness, did not escape me, nor did it entice any of the party to comment.

The topic of a prospective ball at Netherfield was broached by Bingley, and Miss Bingley, perhaps seeking to divert the conversation from its current stagnation, questioned the prudence of such an event. Her challenge to her brother's intentions was met with a lighthearted rebuke, as Bingley remained steadfast in his desire to host the assembly once Jane's health permitted.

It was then that the evening took a more curious turn, as Miss Bingley invited Elizabeth to take a turn about the room with her. This subtle strategy was not lost on me; Miss Bingley's aim was clear—to draw my notice, perhaps to incite some reaction or feeling. Elizabeth's compliance with the request was gracious, and the two ladies began their promenade. Their movement attracted my attention, causing me to close my book and observe their discourse.

Miss Bingley's subsequent efforts to engage me further were relentless, yet it was Elizabeth's perception of my reluctance that truly captured the moment. "Not at all," she replied to Miss Bingley's confusion over my reticence. "But depend upon it, he means to be severe on us, and our surest way of disappointing him will be to ask nothing about it."

Miss Bingley, ever tenacious, sought to continue the engagement, her playful chastisement of my words prompting Elizabeth to suggest that the best course of action would be to tease and laugh at me. Her jest was met with a smile, though I could not fully participate in their mirth, my mind preoccupied with the implications of our exchange.

The discussion that ensued was one of playful banter and veiled truths, a dance of words that revealed as much as it concealed. Elizabeth's ease in deflecting Miss Bingley's provocations and my own guarded yet candid responses created a tapestry of conversation that was as intricate as it was revealing.

The conversation continued, touching upon the qualities of pride and vanity, the virtues and vices of character, and the permanence of my good opinion once lost. Elizabeth's response to my admission was both poignant and playful, an intricate dance of words that left an indelible impression upon me.

As the evening wore on, and Miss Bingley, tiring of her own game,, called for music to fill the silence, I found myself reflecting on the events of the night. The danger of paying Elizabeth too much attention was becoming increasingly clear to me, yet the pull of her presence was undeniable.

Retiring to my study, I was left to ponder the revelations of the evening. The interplay of affection and rivalry, the veiled motivations of those around me, and the enigma that is Elizabeth Bennet—all these elements combined to create a portrait of a society both confined and confounded by its own expectations.

In the quiet of my solitude, I contemplated the nature of my own character, the pride that defines me, and the growing realization that Elizabeth's opinion, her laughter, and her approbation have begun to hold a value to me that I cannot easily dismiss. As I pen this entry, I am acutely aware that my world, once so ordered and predictable, is shifting in ways I am only beginning to understand.

Fitzwilliam Darcy

November 24, 1811

The day dawned with a sense of expectancy, as arrangements were made concerning the departure of the Misses Bennet from Netherfield. Elizabeth, it seemed, was most eager to return to Longbourn, and thus penned a letter to her mother requesting the carriage. The response received did not align with her wishes; Mrs. Bennet, having anticipated a longer visit, dictated that the carriage would not be available until Tuesday.

It was with a certain measure of disquietude that I observed the unfolding of these plans. For while the prospect of their prolonged stay was met with professions of concern and hospitable wishes by the others, I found myself wrestling with a contradictory sentiment—relief at the news of their imminent departure, yet disturbed by the realization of how deeply Miss Elizabeth Bennet had managed to unsettle me.

The interactions of the day were marked by subtleties of expression and veiled intentions. Miss Bingley's regret at the delay she had instigated was palpable, her jealousy and distaste for Elizabeth overshadowing her supposed affection for Jane. Bingley, ever the congenial host, expressed genuine dismay at the prospect of an early parting, his attentions to Jane sincere and persistent.

As for myself, the intelligence of their leaving was met with a complex mixture of satisfaction and undeniable regret. Elizabeth had, in her brief stay, provoked in me a fascination that I was determined to master. Her presence, her lively spirit, and the intellectual challenge she posed were more alluring than I cared to admit. Yet, it was the propriety of distance and the preservation of my own designs that necessitated her absence.

My resolve to maintain a strict distance from her was put to the test, and I found myself exerting a considerable effort to remain detached. On Saturday, though an opportunity presented itself for discourse, I adhered with unwavering discipline to my reading, allowing not even the slightest glance to betray my inner conflict.

The Sabbath brought with it the anticipated separation. The civility of Miss Bingley towards Elizabeth, once tempered with coldness, now seemed to warm as the moment of farewell approached. Her renewed affections for Jane were expressed with an eagerness that bordered on the excessive, yet it was the handshake she offered Elizabeth that marked a notable shift in her manner.

Elizabeth, for her part, departed with a spirit undampened by the events of the visit. Her farewell was lively, her mood elevated, as if the weight of Netherfield's expectations and the intricacies of its social labyrinth were of no consequence to her. Her light-heartedness in the face of such a departure was a trait I could not help but admire, even as I grappled with my own thoughts.

As the carriage pulled away, carrying the Bennet sisters back to the familiarity of their home, I was left to reflect on the impact of their visit. The house, once filled with the vitality of their presence, now resumed its former tranquility, a tranquility that seemed all too silent.

Retreating to the quiet of my own chambers, I contemplated the events of the past week. The daily rhythms of Netherfield, the laughter and conversations shared, the subtle glances and unspoken words—all had been altered by the presence of Elizabeth Bennet. Her departure, while restoring the order of my existence, left an imprint that would not soon be effaced.

In the solitude of my study, I was forced to acknowledge that Elizabeth's influence had reached deeper than I had anticipated. The prospect of not seeing her again brought with it an unexpected sense of loss, a realization that the walls I had erected around my sentiments were perhaps not as impervious as I had believed.

As I pen this entry, I am aware that the coming days will be a test of my resolve. My admiration for her, while real and profound, must be tempered by the demands of my position and the expectations of my society. Yet, Elizabeth Bennet has emerged as a figure unlike any other, challenging my convictions and stirring within me a curiosity that is as unsettling as it is undeniable.

Fitzwilliam Darcy

November 26, 1811

It is with a peculiar sense of disquiet that I commit to paper the events and reflections of this day. The tranquility of Netherfield, so recently restored by the departure of the Misses Bennet, has been disturbed by news from Longbourn that sets the mind into a most uncomfortable agitation.

This morning, as I took my usual repose in the library, a letter arrived from Charles to his sisters, conveying the local news and social ongoings of the Bennets' household. Among the various items of interest, one piece of intelligence captured the immediate attention of all present: the arrival of a certain Mr. Collins at Longbourn and his apparent intentions towards Miss Elizabeth Bennet.

Mr. Collins, I am to understand, is a cousin to the Bennets and stands to inherit the estate due to the entail. It seems the gentleman has taken it upon himself to seek reconciliation with the family through an offer of marriage to one of the daughters. The notion that Elizabeth, with her lively mind and independent spirit, could be the object of such a man's pursuit is a circumstance I find most vexing.

Miss Bingley, ever eager to seize upon any opportunity to disparage Elizabeth, could hardly conceal her mirth at the prospect. "Can you imagine our dear Eliza married to a clergyman?" she exclaimed with a sneer. "A man of such little consequence and, I dare say, even less sense!"

Her words, though intended to provoke, could not rouse me to join in her ridicule. Instead, I found myself inwardly recoiling at the thought of Elizabeth bound to a man who could neither appreciate her intellect nor match her character. It was a match that seemed to me as ill-suited as it was mercenary.

The rest of the morning passed in a blur of activity and idle chatter, but my thoughts remained preoccupied with the unwelcome news. In the solitude of my chamber, I reflected upon my interactions with Elizabeth. Her image, her words, and the subtle expressions of her countenance during our recent encounters were vivid in my memory, and I could not dismiss the concern I felt at the notion of her being linked to Mr. Collins.

What Mr. Collins might offer in terms of security, he would undoubtedly lack in companionship and understanding. Elizabeth deserves a partner who would engage with her fully, who would challenge and be challenged by her keen wit and insightful observations.

I cannot deny that my own feelings towards Elizabeth are complex and, perhaps, still evolving. The knowledge that her hand may soon be promised to another has stirred within me a discomposure I am reluctant to examine too closely. It is a matter of internal conflict, for while I am yet convinced that a connection with the Bennet family would be imprudent, I find the idea of Elizabeth united with Mr. Collins to be most disconcerting.

The day wanes, and I am left to ponder the strange course of human affections. How is it that the heart can be so drawn to what the mind finds so ill-advised? Elizabeth Bennet has become a figure of considerable import in my thoughts, and the prospect of her engagement, regardless of whom it is to, has revealed to me the extent to which she has occupied my considerations.

As I look out over the fading light of the Netherfield grounds, I am resolved to maintain my composure and propriety. Yet, I cannot help but wonder what role, if any, I might play in the narrative unfolding at Longbourn. For now, I must content myself with the role of a distant observer, but the future, as ever, remains shrouded in uncertainty.

Fitzwilliam Darcy

November 28, 1811

The morning was of a character that suggested tranquility, the gentle clatter of hooves on cobblestones the only intrusion upon the stillness that had settled over Netherfield. It was with a mind preoccupied by recent events that I accompanied Bingley on his ride towards Longbourn. His purpose was clear—to inquire after Miss Jane Bennet's health—and I, his steadfast companion, could scarce object to the civility of such a gesture.

As we navigated the familiar thoroughfares of Meryton, our path converged with a group of ladies, among whom were the Misses Bennet. Bingley, ever amiable and attentive, engaged them directly with the grace and affability that are the hallmarks of his character. He expressed his intent to visit Longbourn, his concern for Miss Bennet's well-being evident in his every word and gesture. I echoed his sentiments with a polite bow, my own gaze carefully measured to avoid lingering on Elizabeth.

It was then, in the midst of these genteel exchanges, that an occurrence transpired which sent a tremor through the facade of cordiality. A stranger approached, and as his eyes met mine, a silent confrontation unfolded—one that was keenly observed by Elizabeth, if her countenance was any indication of her surprise.

The gentleman was Mr. Wickham, a figure from my past whose presence here was as unexpected as it was unwelcome. Our mutual recognition was marked by a shift in demeanor; he, with a touch of his hat, and I, barely acknowledging the gesture. The moment was fraught with a tension that belied the simplicity of our salutations.

Elizabeth's astonishment at our exchange did not escape my notice, nor could it. Her curiosity was palpable, a mirror to the confusion that must have been etched upon my own features. What thoughts passed through her mind at the sight of such an encounter, I could not say, but her desire to understand was unmistakable.

Bingley, bless his heart, seemed oblivious to the undercurrents of the moment. His focus remained singularly on Jane, and with a polite farewell, he guided our departure, leaving Meryton and its inhabitants behind. As we continued back towards Netherfield, I was grateful for the distraction provided by the rhythm of the ride and the necessity of polite conversation.

Yet, as the landscape passed by, I could not shake the disquiet that Mr. Wickham's appearance had stirred within me. His presence in the county, his proximity to Elizabeth and her family, was a development that required consideration. The history between Wickham and myself was a sordid one, fraught with deceit and regret, and the thought of Elizabeth being drawn into its orbit was a source of great unease.

The remainder of the day was spent at Netherfield, walking the grounds and taking care of business matters, at dinner the conversation light, yet the shadow of the morning's encounter loomed large in my thoughts.

It was not until my return to my quarters that I had the opportunity to reflect fully upon the day's events. In the quiet of my study, I contemplated the implications of Wickham's arrival in the area, the potential for gossip and scandal, and the necessity of guarding against any interference he might pose to the well-being of those I—against my better judgment—had come to regard with a degree of concern.

As I pen this entry, I am resolute in my determination to protect not only my own reputation but also that of the Bennet family from the machinations of a man as unscrupulous as Wickham. How I am to accomplish this without revealing the full extent of our shared history is a challenge I have yet to resolve.

The image of Elizabeth's startled expression remains with me—a reminder of the complexities of human interaction and the unpredictable nature of life's encounters. Her opinion, her estimations of character, are of an importance to me that I had not anticipated, and the desire to shield her from Wickham's influence is a compulsion I cannot easily dismiss.

Fitzwilliam Darcy

November 30, 1811

The immensity of Netherfield Park is today dwarfed by the looming festivity that will soon inhabit its halls. Invitations, penned with meticulous care, have been sent to every family of standing within the vicinity, and the house is now a symphony of industrious preparation for the ball. Each room is undergoing a transformation, with staff members fluttering from task to task like bees in a hive.

Yet amidst this bustle, my thoughts turn inward, and I find myself seeking solace in the quiet companionship of my journal. It is here that I confess a turmoil that rivals any social whirlwind: the complicated musings of my heart regarding Miss Elizabeth Bennet.

In a moment of introspection, I have penned a letter to Georgiana, my dear sister, whose gentle wisdom has often been my guiding star. I have laid bare before her the depth of my admiration for Elizabeth, a sentiment that I am coming to realize may well exceed the boundaries of mere esteem. Yet, the specter of prudence looms – her family's station, their connections, or lack thereof, are considerations that cannot be dismissed by a man in my position.

The Bingley sisters have voiced their concerns over the guest list for the ball, lamenting the necessity of entertaining individuals they deem socially inferior. Charles, ever the embodiment of amiability, has countered their objections with good-natured remonstrance, advocating for a spirit of inclusivity and conviviality that I find myself envying.

The ball at Netherfield presents itself as an opportunity for me to observe Miss Bennet anew, to witness her amongst her peers, and perhaps to glean further insight into the nature of my own affections. I cannot deny a certain eagerness for this event, a chance to be in her presence once more.

I now await Georgiana's reply with a sense of expectancy, for her thoughts carry weight and often bring clarity to my own. Her response will no doubt provide the counsel I require, as I navigate this uncharted territory of emotion and duty.

As the evening draws near, I will endeavor to conduct myself with the decorum expected of a man of my standing. Yet, I cannot help but wonder if the night will bring with it revelations that may alter the course of my future considerations.

For now, I remain in a state of anticipation, the quiet scratch of my pen a stark contrast to the cacophony of preparation that surrounds me. It is a curious state of being – to be so surrounded, yet so profoundly alone with one's thoughts.

Fitzwilliam Darcy

December 1, 1811

As I sit to recount this evening's occurrences at the Netherfield ball, the quiet of my chamber stands in stark contrast to the whirl of music and conversation that filled the hours before. The event was to be the pinnacle of Netherfield's social engagements, and yet, for me, it unfolded as a tableau of disquieting revelations and encounters which have left me in a state of considerable reflection.

The drawing-room was aglow with the flicker of candles and the bright colors of gowns and uniforms as the guests assembled, a milieu of local society. Miss Elizabeth Bennet entered with a countenance of such anticipation that it could not escape notice. Her eyes scanned the assembly, searching, I discerned, for Mr. Wickham. I observed her reaction when his absence became apparent – a mixture of confusion and a dawning displeasure that did not elude my perception.

It became known through the murmurs of the crowd and the pointed words of Mr. Denny that Wickham's absence was no accident but a deliberate avoidance. Elizabeth's distress was palpable, and I could not help but feel a twinge of responsibility, though I had no hand in his decision to absent himself.

The evening progressed, and I found myself in the unexpected position of engaging Miss Bennet for a dance. Her acceptance surprised us both, and I retreated to collect my thoughts, which were in disarray. Her cousin, Mr. Collins, provided a brief interlude of diversion with his comical display of dancing, but my mind was elsewhere, preoccupied with the impending dance with Elizabeth.

When the moment arrived, and I approached her, I could see the reluctance masked behind her polite smile. We took to the floor in silence, the eyes of the room upon us. The dance began, and the silence stretched on, a testament to the chasm between us. Elizabeth, in a move that betrayed her nerves, initiated a trifling conversation about the dance, to which I replied, and then we fell into silence once more.

It was not until she inquired about our previous meeting in Meryton and the formation of a new acquaintance that the conversation took a turn. The mention of Wickham brought a visible change to my demeanor; I felt a coldness settle over me, and though I wished to remain indifferent, I could not. My response was measured but carried a weight of meaning that hinted at the truth of my sentiments towards the man.

"Mr. Wickham is blessed with such happy manners as may insure his making friends; whether he may be equally capable of retaining them, is less certain."

"He has been so unlucky as to lose your friendship," replied Elizabeth, with emphasis, "and in a manner which he is likely to suffer from all his life."

The dance concluded, and we parted – I, with a mind burdened by the complexities of my feelings towards her and the situation at hand; she, no doubt, with her own set of vexations and concerns. The rest of the evening saw me observing her from a distance, noting her interactions with others and her attempts to regain composure.

Mr. Collins, steadfast in his misguided resolution, proceeded to approach me with a confidence that bordered on the absurd.

The scene that unfolded was one I shall not soon forget. Mr. Collins, with a solemnity that belied the awkwardness of his position, delivered what can only be described as a tribute to Lady Catherine, replete with assurances of her good health and references to his own rectitude. I endured this address with a composure that was tested by the length and content of his speech. My response, though polite, was terse, and I excused myself at the earliest opportunity, leaving Mr. Collins to ponder the interaction.

Miss Elizabeth's reaction to her cousin's behaviour was a mixture of dismay and embarrassment, which I observed from a distance. Mr. Collins, upon returning to her side, seemed utterly oblivious to the impropriety of his conduct, instead expressing satisfaction with the civility of my response. His interpretation of the exchange, and his apparent pleasure in it, struck me as delusional, a testament to his vanity and lack of discernment.

The incident has left me with much to consider. It is clear that Mr. Collins' association with Lady Catherine will inevitably lead to further entanglement, and the prospect of him becoming connected to Elizabeth through marriage is one I find increasingly distressing. The disparity in their characters and sensibilities could not be more pronounced, and the thought of Elizabeth bound to such a man is intolerable.

Furthermore, the interactions of the evening have underscored the growing complexity of my feelings towards Miss Elizabeth Bennet. Despite the impropriety of her family and the unsuitability of a match, I find my thoughts returning to her with an intensity that both confounds and disturbs me. Her intelligence, her spirited nature, and the liveliness of her expression have imprinted themselves upon me, challenging the very principles I have long upheld.

As the night wanes and the revelry of the ball becomes a memory, I am left to grapple with these revelations in the solitude of my study. The path ahead is uncertain, and the propriety of my future actions is a matter of considerable debate within my own mind. For now, I must content myself with the reflection that this evening has brought to light feelings and considerations that will require careful examination in the days to come.

Fitzwilliam Darcy

December 2, 1811

The morning after the ball found Netherfield abuzz with the echoes of the previous evening's revelry. As I sit here, recounting the events in the solitude of my chamber, I am compelled to confront not only the gaiety but also the distasteful aftermath that unfolded this morning.

The breakfast room was a scene of animated discussion, with Miss Bingley and Mrs. Hurst leading a critique of the Bennet family that was as spirited as it was uncharitable. Their ridicule spared not the mother, whose manners and lack of decorum were the subject of much scorn, nor the younger sisters, whose exuberance was deemed wild and unbecoming of young ladies of genteel birth. Even Mr. Collins, with his fawning obsequiousness and absurd speech, was a target of their derision.

Their words, though perhaps not without some merit in observation, left a bitter taste. As I listened, my mind wandered to Elizabeth, whose intelligence and grace stood in stark contrast to the behavior of her relations. It was a dichotomy that pained me, for I could not deny the truth in some of their jibes, yet I found the cruelty with which they were delivered to be distasteful.

Miss Bingley, in particular, was relentless. "Can you imagine, Mr. Darcy," she said with a sardonic smile, "such a family connected to you? The very thought is laughable. The mother, a woman so lacking in propriety, the sisters so decidedly common, and Mr. Collins—can there be a more pitiable creature?"

Her comments elicited laughter from the others, but I remained silent, my thoughts consumed by the unfairness of Elizabeth being judged by the actions of her relations. The mirth of the company seemed to me a cruel sport, and I found myself more and more at odds with their sentiments.

I attempted to steer the conversation to less disparaging topics, but the damage was done. The image of Elizabeth at the ball, dancing with grace and conversing with wit, stood in stark contrast to the picture painted by the Bingley sisters. It was a comparison that troubled me deeply, for I knew that in their eyes, and indeed in the eyes of society, the family one belonged to was often more important than the individual's own merits.

The merriment of the previous evening now seemed a distant memory, overshadowed by the realization that my own struggle between affection and propriety was a reflection of a larger societal conflict. The Bennet family, with all their flaws and lack of connections, were a barrier to my burgeoning feelings for Elizabeth that I could not easily dismiss.

As the conversation continued, I found myself withdrawing inward, contemplating the future and the choices that lay before me. The laughter and mockery of the company rang hollow, and I felt an increasing sense of isolation from their views.

This journal entry serves as a testament to the internal turmoil that plagues me. The collision of my feelings for Elizabeth with the expectations of my station has left me in a state of disquiet that I fear will not be easily resolved. The path ahead is fraught with challenges, and I must navigate it with care, lest my actions betray my heart or my duty.

The day is waning, and I am left to ponder the complexity of my circumstances. The Bennet family, for all their perceived shortcomings, have produced a daughter who has captivated me in ways I never thought possible. It is a conundrum that I must endeavor to understand, and my reflections on this matter will no doubt occupy much of my thoughts in the days to come.

Fitzwilliam Darcy

December 3, 1811

In the quietude of my study at Netherfield, I find myself compelled to note down the extraordinary events of this day, which have given rise to a myriad of emotions within me. The morning brought with it a revelation that has since occupied my every thought and colored my perceptions most profoundly.

As I took my usual place at the breakfast table, Charles, with his characteristic good cheer, broached a subject that caught me entirely unawares. "Darcy," he began with a bemused expression, "you will hardly credit it, but Mr. Collins has made an offer of marriage to Miss Elizabeth Bennet!"

I must confess that upon hearing these words, I experienced an immediate and visceral reaction, a mixture of alarm and—dare I say—relief, as he continued, "And imagine our surprise when we learned that she refused him!"

The news of Elizabeth's refusal sent an inexplicable surge of satisfaction through me, though I was quick to mask my emotions beneath a veneer of indifference. I inquired as to the particulars of the refusal, to which Bingley responded with a shrug, "It appears that Miss

Bennet does not find Mr. Collins' situation and connections sufficient motivation for matrimony."

His words struck a chord within me, for they echoed a sentiment I have often entertained in my quieter moments—that Elizabeth Bennet was a woman of deep feeling and discernment, not easily swayed by convenience or duty. The realization that she had acted in accordance with her true feelings filled me with an admiration that I could scarcely admit to myself.

Yet the conversation took another turn when Bingley, with a chuckle, imparted the subsequent development: "But fear not for Mr. Collins, for he has found solace in the arms of another! Miss Lucas has accepted his proposal with all the expediency one could wish for."

The news of Charlotte Lucas's engagement to Mr. Collins was met with a range of reactions around the table, from amusement to disbelief. I, however, found myself reflecting upon the pragmatism of Miss Lucas's decision and the stark contrast it presented to Elizabeth's refusal.

As I sit here now, the quiet of the room is a balm to the tumult of my thoughts. The knowledge of Elizabeth's refusal has confirmed in me a belief in her virtues and the depth of her character. Yet, I am also aware that her actions have further complicated the already intricate web of my feelings for her.

The idea that she could so decidedly reject Mr. Collins, a man whose connections to Lady Catherine de Bourgh might offer her some material advantage, suggests a strength of will and a purity of motive that I cannot help but admire. It speaks to a shared value, a disdain for marriages built on convenience rather than affection—a value I find increasingly important.

The remainder of the day passed in a haze of contemplation as I considered the implications of these events. Elizabeth's refusal has, in some indefinable way, altered the tenor of my thoughts regarding her.

It has also brought into sharp relief the challenges that any potential union between us would face.

As night draws near, I am left with a profound sense of uncertainty about the future. The course of my own actions seems less clear to me now, as I weigh the dictates of my heart against the expectations of my society and station.

In the solitude of these pages, I can admit to a feeling of closeness to Elizabeth Bennet that is both exhilarating and deeply disconcerting. Her refusal of Mr. Collins has, paradoxically, both widened the gulf between us and drawn me nearer to her in spirit.

Fitzwilliam Darcy

December 5, 1811

It is with a heavy hand that I set my pen to paper this evening, for the events of this day have been of such significance that their weight lingers upon my shoulders. The quietude of my chambers provides a stark contrast to the tumultuous deliberations that have occupied the majority of our waking hours here at Netherfield.

The matter at hand was the disposition of my dear friend Charles Bingley's affections towards Miss Jane Bennet, and the perceived inequality of their attachment. It was a subject broached with the utmost trepidation, for the happiness of a friend is not a matter to be interceded upon lightly. Yet, after long observation and much contemplation, it became apparent to me, as well as to Miss Bingley and Mrs. Hurst, that while Charles's affections were deeply engaged, Miss Bennet's appeared far more reserved, if not entirely placid.

It is a painful thing to sow seeds of doubt in the fertile ground of a friend's romantic aspirations, but it is a cruelty greater still to allow him to pursue a course that may lead to his undoing. Thus, with the greatest care and a sense of solemn duty, I expressed to Charles my observations and the concerns that had arisen therefrom.

"Charles," I began, with a gravity befitting the discussion, "you are aware of my esteem for you and my desire for your lifelong happiness. It is for this reason alone that I must convey my observations concerning Miss Bennet. While none can question her amiability, it is uncertain whether her feelings for you are as fervent as your own. It would be a grave injustice to yourself to be connected to a woman whose heart is not equally engaged."

Miss Bingley, ever more direct in her approach, added her own sentiments, underscoring the social repercussions that might arise from such an unequal match. "Consider, dear brother," she urged, "the lack of propriety displayed by Miss Bennet's family, and the imprudence of allying yourself with connections so decidedly inferior to our own."

Charles, whose countenance had grown increasingly troubled, listened with a pained expression. "I had hoped," he said, his voice tinged with a forlorn note, "that the sincerity of my regard for Jane might overcome such obstacles."

Yet, as the conversation progressed, it became clear that the strength of our arguments and the evidence of Miss Bennet's reserved demeanor had made an impression upon him. It was decided, with a heaviness of spirit, that a departure from Netherfield would be prudent, allowing Charles time and distance to consider his feelings and the potential consequences of his attachment.

The Bingley sisters, taking it upon themselves to communicate our imminent departure, penned a letter to Miss Bennet. The epistle conveyed, with all due civility, that we were to leave for London and that Charles's return to Hertfordshire was not to be anticipated in the near future. The task of writing such a letter was not taken lightly, and it was dispatched with an awareness of the disappointment it would surely cause.

As I retire for the evening, I am beset by a disquiet that I cannot easily dispel. The necessity of our actions today, while clear in the light of reason, sits uneasily upon my conscience. I cannot help but consider the parallel between Charles's situation and my own growing attachment to Elizabeth, an attachment that I have endeavored to conceal even from myself.

The impending journey to London provides an opportunity for reflection, a chance to distance myself from the source of my own conflicting emotions. Yet, I suspect that the miles that will soon lie between Elizabeth and me will do little to diminish the impression she has made upon my heart.

It is in these quiet moments of solitude that I am forced to confront the possibility that in striving to protect my friend from a match that could bring him discomfort, I have inadvertently highlighted the very struggle that lies within my own breast.

Fitzwilliam Darcy

December 6, 1811

Today, we bid adieu to Netherfield, the place that has been the stage for so many varied scenes in these past months. The carriages were loaded under a stark grey sky that seemed to reflect the somber mood of our party, or perhaps it was merely my own spirits that painted such a hue upon the day.

As we set out for London, the countryside of Hertfordshire receded behind us, with its rolling hills and familiar roads giving way to the more imposing and less forgiving landscape of the city. Charles sat opposite me, his usual vivacity dimmed by the recent events, and it was not long before Caroline, with her penchant for teasing, sought to lift his spirits with a barb wrapped in jest.

"Oh, Charles," she began, her voice dripping with false sympathy, "to be parted from Miss Bennet! How shall you find the strength to endure such a trial?"

Her words, though light in tone, struck a chord, and Charles, with a rueful smile, replied, "Indeed, Caroline, you must allow me my feelings. They are not so easily set aside."

The banter continued, and soon Caroline's attentions turned to me, her eyes alight with mischief. "And you, Mr. Darcy," she cooed, "how will you survive without the pleasure of gazing into Miss Elizabeth Bennet's fine eyes?"

Her question, intended to provoke, instead sent a jolt through me, for the thought of Elizabeth and the prospect of not seeing her again was one I had been resolutely avoiding. Maintaining my composure, I answered with a coolness I did not entirely feel. "I assure you, Miss Bingley, that I am quite capable of managing my own affairs without the need for such distractions."

Yet, as we journeyed on, the image of Elizabeth, her eyes so expressive and lively, remained etched in my mind, a reminder of what I was leaving behind. The conversation in the carriage turned to other matters, but a part of me remained in Hertfordshire, in the company of a woman whose image I could not, and perhaps did not wish to, escape.

The hours passed, and London greeted us with its cacophony and bustle, a stark contrast to the relative peace of the country. We settled into our respective abodes, the Bingleys to their townhouse and I to my own. The evening brought solitude and the opportunity for reflection.

As I sit now, penning these words, I am forced to confront the disquiet in my heart. The decision to persuade Charles away from Jane Bennet was made with the best of intentions, yet I cannot shake the feeling that in doing so, I have somehow betrayed my own desires.

The distance between Elizabeth and myself may be measured in miles, but the true expanse that separates us is one of social expectations and familial duty. It is a chasm that seems insurmountable, and yet the thought of never seeing her again fills me with a sense of loss that is difficult to articulate.

The days ahead will no doubt be filled with the demands of city life and the expectations of my station, but the memory of Elizabeth, her intelligence, her wit, and yes, her fine eyes, will accompany me.

They serve as a constant reminder of what I have left behind and of the questions that yet linger in my heart.

Fitzwilliam Darcy

January 23, 1812

The passage of time in London has done little to diminish the constancy of my thoughts as they drift back to Hertfordshire and the events that transpired at Netherfield. The city, with all its diversions and social obligations, cannot seem to fully engage my attention, for there is a restlessness within me that I find difficult to soothe.

Today's entry is marked by a development that has caused a considerable degree of inner conflict. Miss Jane Bennet, the elder sister of Elizabeth, has come to London, accompanied by her Aunt Gardiner. It seems that the purpose of her visit is at least, in part, to be near Charles, who remains unaware of her presence in the city.

Miss Bingley, upon learning of Miss Bennet's arrival, has taken it upon herself to ensure that her brother remains ignorant of this fact. She insists that it is for his own good, to protect him from an attachment that could only bring him discomfort and social disadvantage. I confess that I have been complicit in this concealment, for while my conscience chides me for the deception, my concern for Charles's welfare echoes Miss Bingley's reasoning.

Yet, I cannot deny that there is another, less noble part of me that is relieved by the distance this secrecy maintains between Charles and the Bennets, for it also serves to keep Elizabeth from my immediate orbit. The very notion that I should find solace in this separation is a matter of great personal reproach.

Miss Bingley's machinations do not end with mere concealment. She has taken active measures to ensure that any attempt by Miss Bennet to call upon us is met with polite excuses and carefully constructed barriers. Her determination to sever the ties between her brother and the Bennet family is unyielding, and I watch her efforts with a mixture of admiration and dismay.

As I reflect upon these actions, I am struck by the complexity of human motives and the intricate web of societal expectations that govern our behavior. We act under the guise of protecting those we care for, and yet our actions can so often be guided by our own desires and prejudices.

The days pass, and I find myself increasingly unsettled. Jane Bennet's quiet dignity in the face of our subtle rejection only serves to heighten my respect for her character, and by extension, that of her sister. I wonder at the justice of our actions, and whether the preservation of social standing is worth the possible sacrifice of genuine affection and happiness.

It is in these quiet hours of the night, as I commit my thoughts to this journal, that I allow myself to ponder the path not taken. What might have been had we encouraged Charles to pursue his heart's desire? And what of my own heart, which, despite all efforts to the contrary, remains inextricably tied to Elizabeth Bennet?

Fitzwilliam Darcy

February 10, 1812

The arrival of my cousin, Colonel Fitzwilliam, in these cold winter weeks has been a most welcome reprieve from the solitude that often accompanies my evenings. His company offers the comfort of family and the ease of a friendship long established by the shared experiences of our youth.

This evening, as we sat by the fire in my study, a fine brandy warming our hands, our conversation turned, as it often does, to matters of the heart and the delicate intricacies of our social engagements. It was in this intimate setting that I found myself confiding in him the part I played in influencing Bingley away from

Miss Jane Bennet, and the subsequent concealment of her presence in London.

The Colonel listened with a steady gaze, his expression one of understanding rather than judgment. "Darcy," he said, his voice steady and calm, "it is a difficult thing to weigh the happiness of a friend against what society might deem a more prudent course."

I nodded, grateful for his acknowledgment of the complexity of the situation. "Indeed," I replied, "and yet, I cannot help but feel that in my caution, I have perhaps overstepped, that I have allowed my concern for the potential imprudence of the match to cloud my judgment."

The Colonel considered this, swirling the brandy in his glass before speaking. "It is a fine line we walk, between guiding those we care for and controlling their fates. But tell me, Darcy, in your efforts to protect Bingley, have you considered the true depth of Miss Bennet's affections? Could it be that you have misjudged her reserve for indifference?"

His question struck at the very heart of my uncertainty. "It is possible," I conceded, feeling the weight of his words. "In truth, I have seen in her a composure and a kindness that speak to a character of no common order. But to admit as much is to acknowledge that I may have erred greatly."

The Colonel nodded, his expression thoughtful. "And what of the lady's sister, Miss Elizabeth Bennet? It seems to me that she occupies more of your thoughts than you might be willing to admit."

I felt a flush of warmth at the mention of her name, a reaction that did not go unnoticed by my cousin. "She is indeed remarkable," I allowed, my voice betraying a hint of the admiration I felt. "Her intelligence and vivacity are qualities that I find... compelling."

A knowing smile touched the Colonel's lips. "Compelling, indeed. It is a rare thing to find a woman who challenges you, Darcy. Perhaps in this case, the heart knows more than the mind would like to acknowledge."

We sat for a few moments in companionable silence, the crackling of the fire the only sound in the room. It was a comfort to speak openly of my doubts and to receive the counsel of someone who knew me well enough to offer wisdom without censure.

As the evening wore on, and the brandy settled warm in our bellies, I felt a sense of gratitude for the Colonel's visit. His presence has provided not only the solace of kinship but also a mirror to reflect upon the choices I have made and the path I have yet to choose.

Fitzwilliam Darcy

March 10, 1812

The chill of winter gives way to the promise of spring as I sit by my desk, the golden light of dawn casting a warm glow upon the letter I have just received from my esteemed Aunt, Lady Catherine. Her words, penned with the expectation of acquiescence, summon me to Rosings Park, that grand edifice of ostentation and familial obligation.

Yet, within the neatly scribed lines of duty and decorum lies another, more compelling call to action. Word has reached me, through channels both direct and serendipitous, that Elizabeth Bennet is to reside at the parsonage in Hunsford for a span of time, a guest of the Collinses. The knowledge of her nearness to Rosings alters the very fabric of my intentions, lending a weight to my aunt's invitation that was heretofore absent.

In the quiet hours of this morning, as I await the Colonel's company for breakfast, I am struck by the duality of my circumstances. The prospect of being in Elizabeth's company once more fills me with a fervent, if not entirely rational, sense of anticipation. Yet, it is a sentiment tempered by the remembrance of the formidable expectations that my aunt harbors regarding her daughter, Anne, and the role I am expected to play in her future.

Lady Catherine's design in pairing me with her daughter has been a constant, albeit subtle, pressure since my youth. Anne, with her delicate health and reserved nature, has always been presented as a suitable match, a union that would consolidate familial ties and estates. My aunt's machinations, while transparent, are not without a certain maternal cunning.

As the Colonel joins me, his countenance cheerful and unburdened by the weight of such expectations, I find myself envious of his freedom. We discuss our impending visit to Rosings, and I am careful to craft my words with a casualness that belies the true depth of my eagerness to see Elizabeth again.

The decision is made; we shall depart for Kent forthwith. The Colonel, ever the soldier, seeks the reprieve of the countryside after the dreariness of winter barracks. As for myself, I cannot deny that the landscapes of Rosings hold little allure compared to the singular pleasure I anticipate in observing Elizabeth once more.

As I seal this entry with wax, I am aware that the days ahead will test the fortitude of my resolve. I must navigate the expectations of my aunt, the attentions she will undoubtedly lavish upon me as a suitor for her daughter, and the pull of my own heart toward a woman whose lively eyes and quick wit have ensnared me more completely than I dare admit.

The stage is set for a sojourn that may well dictate the course of my future, for better or for worse. How I shall comport myself in the face of these challenges is a matter for the fates to decide. My only hope is that, in the end, I may act with honor and integrity, even as the tempest of my emotions threatens to steer me off course.

Fitzwilliam Darcy

March 31, 1812

The morning air was crisp as we departed for Rosings, the carriage wheels crunching on the gravel. I was acutely aware that Elizabeth Bennet's proximity at the parsonage would soon bring about a meeting, the anticipation of which caused an unfamiliar restlessness in my otherwise composed demeanor. Colonel Fitzwilliam seemed to sense my tension, offering a distraction through light-hearted conversation, yet my thoughts were singularly occupied.

Upon our arrival at the parsonage, Mr. Collins greeted us with the obsequious flattery I have come to expect. His pride at our attendance was palpable, and he hastened to inform us of Elizabeth's presence within. My heart quickened at the mention of her name, though I endeavored to maintain an outward appearance of indifference.

As we were announced and entered the modest drawing-room, I saw her amongst the small assembly. She was as I remembered—her fine eyes sparking with intelligence, her manner at once composed and inviting. The exchange of courtesies was brief, Elizabeth's courtesy to me marked by the same reserve that I myself projected.

The conversation flowed more readily from Colonel Fitzwilliam, whose easy manners endeared him to our hosts. I, on the other hand, found myself momentarily at a loss, the usual flow of society's pleasantries escaping me in her presence. It was only after a time that I inquired after the health of her family, a question that served as a veil for my deeper concern for her well-being.

Her response was expected, but her following remark struck a chord of guilt within me. "My eldest sister has been in town these three months. Have you never happened to see her there?" The inquiry, innocent as it was, felt like a probe to my very conscience, knowing full well the role I had played in concealing Jane's presence from Bingley. I could not discern if Elizabeth was aware of the depth of my involvement, but the momentary falter in my response may have betrayed more than I intended.

As we took our leave, the image of Elizabeth's inquisitive eyes lingered with me, prompting a reflection on the justice of my past actions.

The days that followed were marked by an air of expectancy. Though Colonel Fitzwilliam visited the parsonage with some frequency, I confined my interactions with Elizabeth to the chance meetings at church, each encounter sending ripples through the calm surface of my life.

When at last the invitation from Lady Catherine arrived, it was with a mixture of relief and trepidation that we entered her imposing drawing-room. Her Ladyship received us with civility, though it was clear that our company was secondary to her desire to boast and preen before her nephews.

Colonel Fitzwilliam, ever the congenial guest, soon found himself engaged in lively discourse with Elizabeth. Their conversation, covering topics from literature to the local scenery, drew the attention of the entire room, including my own. I could not help but observe them, a mixture of admiration and something akin to jealousy stirring within me.

Lady Catherine, never one to be excluded, interjected with her usual imperiousness, demanding inclusion in their exchange. The talk of music led to an invitation for Elizabeth to play, and she obliged, taking her place at the pianoforte with a grace that captivated the room.

As I watched her perform, the sound of the music seemed secondary to the sight of her hands moving deftly across the keys, her expression one of focused serenity. When invited by Colonel Fitzwilliam to join her, I moved with measured steps, positioning myself to better appreciate her talent, though my true intent was to be near her.

Our conversation, once begun, was filled with the familiar banter that had come to define our interactions. Her playful accusations regarding my behavior in Hertfordshire brought forth laughter, yet behind the jest lay truths that resonated within us both. I found her courage and candor disarming, and in her company, I allowed a glimpse of my genuine self to show—a self that was increasingly drawn to the spirited woman before me.

Lady Catherine's interruption to extol her own unexercised musical talents and to offer unsolicited advice was a reminder of the expectations that surrounded me. Yet, as I observed Elizabeth navigate my aunt's overbearing critique with civility and poise, my respect for her only deepened.

As the evening drew to a close, I found myself reluctant to part from the parsonage and the enchanting company within. The journey back to Rosings was made in silence, my thoughts a tumult of emotions that I could scarcely comprehend. It was clear to me now that Elizabeth Bennet had become an indelible presence in my life, one that challenged the very foundations of my beliefs and desires.

Fitzwilliam Darcy

April 1, 1812

A morning of peculiar unrest beckoned me from the imposing walls of Rosings to the humble abode of Mr. Collins. The walk, intended to clear my thoughts, became a pilgrimage of a different sort as I approached the parsonage. I anticipated a morning of polite, if not tiresome, conversation with the Collinses and their guest, Miss Elizabeth Bennet. Yet, fate, it seems, had conspired to set a different scene.

Upon my entrance, I found Miss Bennet alone, an unexpected circumstance that arrested my composure and set my heart to an uncharacteristic flutter. My intrusion startled her, and in my disconcertment, I stumbled over my words, offering an apology as I explained my mistaken understanding that all the ladies were within.

There we sat, two solitary figures bound by propriety yet divided by an invisible chasm of unspoken thoughts and emotions. Our initial exchanges concerning Rosings were perfunctory at best, and it was not long before an oppressive silence threatened to engulf us both. It was absolutely necessary to find some common ground upon which to converse.

In a moment of impulsive curiosity, I broached the subject of our sudden departure from Netherfield. "How very suddenly you all quitted Netherfield last November, Mr. Darcy!" she remarked. "It must have been a most agreeable surprise to Mr. Bingley to see you all after him so soon; for, if I recollect right, he went but the day before."

My response was terse, "Perfectly so, I thank you," yet I could feel the weight of her unasked questions pressing upon me.

She continued, pressing the matter further, "I think I have understood that Mr. Bingley has not much idea of ever returning to Netherfield again?"

The question hung heavily between us, and I replied with calculated ambiguity, "I have never heard him say so; but it is probable that he may spend very little of his time there in future."

The topic shifted to the felicity of Mr. Collins's marriage, and I found myself praising the union with a sincerity I had not expected to voice. "Mr. Collins appears very fortunate in his choice of a wife," I ventured.

"Yes, indeed; his friends may well rejoice in his having met with one of the very few sensible women who would have accepted him, or have made him happy if they had," she replied with a perceptiveness that spoke of a deep understanding of her friend's circumstances.

As our conversation meandered from the merits of matrimony to the considerations of distance and family, I found myself drawn deeper into the labyrinth of her intellect and wit. Her observations on the relative nature of distance prompted a smile from me, for there was an unspoken acknowledgment of the vast social gulf that lay between us.

"You cannot have a right to such very strong local attachment," I remarked, inadvertently betraying my awareness of her thoughts on Jane and Netherfield.

The ensuing dialogue, filled with the subtle barbs and parries of our unique rapport, served to remind me of the singular nature of our acquaintance. We danced around truths known only to ourselves, each word laced with layers of meaning and sentiment.

Yet, as the conversation progressed, I became acutely aware of the impropriety of our seclusion. The sudden entrance of Mrs. Collins and her sister brought an abrupt end to our tête-à-tête. My leave was taken shortly thereafter, with the echo of our exchange resonating within me, a haunting melody of what might have been and what was yet to come.

Upon my return to Rosings, the solitude of my chambers offered little respite from the turmoil of my thoughts. Miss Bennet's presence had become a fixed point in my existence, a star by which I unwittingly navigated. The revelation of my own vulnerability, laid bare in the quietude of the parsonage, was both a torment and an epiphany.

I closed my eyes, and her image was there—indelible, unbidden, and utterly beguiling. The realization of my predicament was as inescapable as it was profound: I was, against all reason and expectation, irrevocably and irretrievably...

Fitzwilliam Darcy

April 10, 1812

The days at Rosings are becoming a sequence of monotonous predictability, interspersed with moments of such acute perplexity that I find myself questioning the very nature of my own heart. My recent encounters with Miss Elizabeth Bennet have only served to deepen the enigma that surrounds my sentiments towards her—a puzzle that becomes more intricate with each passing day.

Charlotte, Elizabeth's friend and now Mrs. Collins, remarked upon my frequent visits to the Parsonage with a teasing insinuation that bespoke an assumption which, though not entirely inaccurate, was still foreign to my own understanding of the situation. "He must be in love with you, or he would never have called on us in this familiar way," she had said to Elizabeth. Yet, the silence that often befalls me in Miss

Bennet's presence could hardly be seen as the behavior of an ardent suitor.

The truth of the matter, as I write these words in the solitude of my chamber, is that my frequent sojourns to the Parsonage are as confounding to me as they are to the inhabitants thereof. I sit there, often in silence, struggling to articulate the myriad thoughts that race through my mind, all while trying to maintain the facade of civility and composure that has become my hallmark.

Colonel Fitzwilliam, with his effortless charm and conviviality, seems to find genuine pleasure in their company—a sentiment, I must confess, I share, though I am loath to reveal it. It is evident that he holds Elizabeth in high regard, and I cannot fault him for his discernment. She is, indeed, a woman of remarkable qualities, and it is with some chagrin that I recognize a tinge of envy at my cousin's ease around her.

As for myself, my appearances at the Parsonage are met with varying degrees of speculation. Mrs. Collins, with a contemplative eye, seems determined to decipher my demeanor—a task I fear is as daunting for her as it is for me. My looks towards Elizabeth, I am told, are the subject of much debate. Are they borne of admiration or merely the vacant stare of a man lost in thought? I cannot say, for my own understanding of my feelings remains shrouded in doubt and uncertainty.

During our walks within the park of Rosings, I have encountered Elizabeth by happenstance—or so it would seem. The frequency of these meetings has led me to question whether some force beyond my control is at play, guiding our steps to converge. Each meeting is more charged than the last, and I have taken to joining her in her ramble, a decision that betrays a longing for her company I am scarcely prepared to admit.

Our conversations during these walks are punctuated by awkward silences and stilted dialogue. I inquire after her satisfaction with her visit, her solitary wanderings, and the Collinses' domestic felicity, all the while aware of the absurdity of my questions. Yet, beneath the banal surface of our discourse lies a current of deeper meaning—an unspoken acknowledgement of the connection that binds us together, despite our best efforts to remain apart.

I have hinted, perhaps too obscurely, at my desire to see her again in Kent, to have her within the sphere of my daily life. The words escape me with a recklessness that I find both alarming and exhilarating. And yet, I cannot discern whether she comprehends the implication of my remarks, or whether she attributes them to some obligation I may feel towards Colonel Fitzwilliam.

The complexity of my own emotions leaves me adrift in a sea of introspection. I am a man divided, caught between the dictates of propriety and the whispers of a heart that seems no longer my own. The more I seek clarity, the more elusive it becomes, and I am left to wonder at the possibility that Elizabeth Bennet has awakened in me a capacity for feeling I had never before imagined.

The hour grows late, and the flickering candle casts shadows upon the page, mirroring the dance of doubt and yearning that occupies my thoughts. What is the nature of this fascination that Miss Bennet has cast over me? It is a question that haunts my waking hours and invades my dreams, leaving me restless and unmoored.

Tomorrow, I will see her again, and perhaps in her presence, I will find the answers that elude me. Or perhaps, I will only find more questions. Either way, I am compelled to follow this path to its inevitable conclusion, wherever it may lead.

Fitzwilliam Darcy

April 15, 1812

In the quiet hours of this April evening, with the gentle hum of Rosings estate as my accompaniment, I find my thoughts preoccupied with a truth I can no longer deny. The solitude of my study offers no respite, for it is in solitude that the heart speaks its most profound truths, and tonight, it speaks of Elizabeth Bennet.

It is with a tumultuous heart and a reluctant hand that I commit to paper an admission that defies the very principles upon which my life has been so meticulously constructed. Despite every rational argument that prudence could muster, despite the chasm of societal standings that lies between us, I am compelled to acknowledge that I am irrevocably, profoundly, and most ardently in love with Miss Elizabeth Bennet.

The realization strikes me with both terror and exhilaration, for in recognizing the depth of my affection, I must also confront the barriers that our disparate ranks impose. She is the daughter of a gentleman, yes, but her family's connections are limited, their social standing precarious at best. My own position, both in society and within my family, demands considerations of propriety and alliance that stand in stark opposition to the dictates of my heart.

Yet, what is rank? What is society's approval when weighed against the stirrings of one's soul? Elizabeth has captivated me not with wealth or status, but with the richness of her mind, the liveliness of her spirit, and the unassuming grace of her manner. Her intelligence challenges me, her candor disarms me, and the light in her eyes when she speaks of her beloved Hertfordshire outshines the grandest chandeliers of Pemberley.

I have watched her, listened to her, and engaged in the delightful warfare of wit that is our unique discourse. Each encounter leaves me more enchanted, more ensnared by the paradox of her being. She is warmth and fire, reason and wildness, pride and vulnerability—all woven into a tapestry more bewitching than any I have ever known.

Yet, alongside this burgeoning love, a sense of dread shadows my every thought. How can I reconcile my feelings with the expectations that have been bestowed upon me since birth? My union with Elizabeth would be met with astonishment and, in some quarters, censure. The specter of familial objection looms large, and the thought of subjecting her to the scrutiny and disdain of those who consider themselves my peers is a torment I cannot easily dismiss.

The specter of duty and the promise of love are at war within me, and I am left to navigate this battlefield with no compass to guide me. How can I offer Elizabeth a future filled with potential strife? How can I deny myself the only woman who has ever stirred the depths of my soul?

I stand at the precipice of a decision that will define the course of my life. To retreat is to consign myself to a future devoid of the one element that has come to mean more to me than any other—her companionship. To advance is to risk the censure of society and the upheaval of all that I have known.

As I close this entry, the weight of my confession heavy upon my heart, I am acutely aware that the path I choose from here will mark a turning point from which there can be no return. Elizabeth Bennet has become the measure by which I judge all happiness, and the thought of a life without her is a prospect too bleak to entertain.

In love, there is no caution, no prudence that can still the yearnings of a heart truly touched. I must face the dawn with the courage to pursue that which I have come to desire above all else—a life shared with Elizabeth. How I shall proceed, I cannot yet say, but proceed I must, for to ignore the call of one's own heart is a fate far worse than any social consequence.

Fitzwilliam Darcy

April 16, 1812

The stark silence of my chamber is a cruel contrast to the tumult that rages within me. I have just returned from the Parsonage, my mind a whirlwind of emotions that I scarcely comprehend, let alone control. This evening's encounter with Miss Elizabeth Bennet—a moment of profound vulnerability and irrevocable truth—has left me undone.

My steps to the Parsonage were those of a man driven by an unseen force, the need to lay bare my heart irresistible. As I approached, my pulse quickened, my thoughts scattered like leaves in the wind. It was a solitary mission; the gravity of my purpose would brook no companionship.

Upon entering the room, her presence struck me like a physical blow. Her form, her face, the very air around her seemed to pull me into an orbit from which I could not, would not, escape. I was resolved to confess my feelings, to declare myself—regardless of the consequences, regardless of the strictures of our respective stations.

The words poured forth from me, a torrent of pent-up emotion that could no longer be contained. "In vain have I struggled. It will not do. My feelings will not be repressed. You must allow me to tell you how ardently I admire and love you."

Her reaction was one of astonishment, a stunned silence that gave me pause. Yet, driven by a force beyond my ken, I continued. I laid before her the full measure of my affection, the struggle against my own better judgment, the acknowledgment of her family's inferiority and how it paled against the strength of my regard.

As I spoke, I was acutely aware of the pride and prejudice that laced my words. I could see the impact in her eyes, the subtle shift of her expression from shock to something far less favorable. My heart, once buoyed by the release of my confession, now felt the leaden weight of her disapprobation.

Her response, when it came, was measured and calm, yet beneath her civility, I sensed a gathering storm. "In such cases as this, it is, I believe, the established mode to express a sense of obligation for the sentiments avowed, however unequally they may be returned."

The ensuing conversation was a blur of pain and clarity. She laid bare before me the depth of her dislike, her disdain for my actions regarding her sister and Mr. Bingley, her abhorrence of my dealings with Mr. Wickham. Each word was a strike against the very essence of my being, a dismantling of the pride I had held so dear.

Yet, it was not her rebuke of my character that wounded me most; it was the unwavering rejection of my suit. To hear that she considered me 'the last man in the world' she could ever be prevailed upon to marry was a torment of the soul I had not thought possible.

I left the Parsonage with her words echoing in my ears, a litany of failures that would haunt me for years to come. The stark realization that I, Fitzwilliam Darcy, had been so thoroughly, so unequivocally rejected, was a bitter draught to swallow.

Now, as I sit and pen these words, the events of the evening replay in my mind with cruel precision. The love that I had confessed—so fervent, so sincere—was met with disdain and accusations. The sharpness of her refusal cuts deeper than any blade.

Had I but approached her with more humility, with a heart unclouded by the arrogance of my position, might the outcome have been different? This question will be my companion in the dark hours to come, a specter that offers no respite.

The journey ahead is unclear. My heart, once so full of hope and resolve, now lies in tatters at my feet. The road to redemption, to self-forgiveness, appears a path steep and treacherous. Yet, it is a path I must endeavor to tread.

The dawn will soon break, bringing with it the light of a new day. But for me, the world has shifted on its axis, and I am left to navigate this altered landscape—a man transformed by love, humbled by rejection, and seeking solace in the knowledge that, though she may not return my affections, my love for Elizabeth Bennet is the truest thing I have ever known.

Fitzwilliam Darcy

April 17, 1812

The morning dawned with a pallor that matched the tumult in my soul. After a night tormented by the specter of Elizabeth's rejection, I rose with a singular determination to address the grievances she so ardently laid against me. The letter I penned to her was both an olive branch and a shield—my final defense against her accusations and my deepest hope to clear my name.

"Be not alarmed, madam, on receiving this letter by the apprehension of its containing any repetition of those sentiments or renewal of those offers which were last night so disgusting to you..."

I wrote without any intention of rousing her displeasure or humbling myself by dwelling on wishes best forgotten. The necessity of clearing my character weighed heavily upon me, and I implored her to grant me her attention, fully aware that it would be bestowed unwillingly.

The grievances she had voiced were two-fold: the part I played in separating Mr. Bingley from her sister and the allegations laid against me by Mr. Wickham. In addressing the former, I did not shy away from acknowledging my role:

"Two offences of a very different nature, and by no means of equal magnitude, you last night laid to my charge..."

I endeavored to explain the separation of Mr. Bingley from Miss Bennet in the most respectful terms, detailing my initial observations of their interactions, which led me to believe her feelings were not engaged as deeply as his. I expressed, with due regard for her feelings, the reasons behind my counsel to Bingley, stressing that it was not solely the lack of advantageous connections that swayed me, but also the behavior of her family that I felt was unbecoming.

Turning to the more painful subject of Mr. Wickham, I laid bare the history of our acquaintance. With a heavy heart, I recounted his duplicity, his dissipated lifestyle, and his attempted elopement with my sister, Georgiana. The details were difficult to commit to paper, for they painted a picture of a man I once considered a friend, now revealed as a scoundrel:

"Mr. Wickham is the son of a very respectable man... his kindness was therefore liberally bestowed..."

I described the provision my father had made for him and the generous legacy left to him, only to be squandered in pursuit of a lifestyle far removed from the clergyman's path he had once pledged to follow.

The letter, though lengthy and painstakingly detailed, was necessary to illuminate the truth of my actions and to dispel the shadows cast upon my character by Wickham's falsehoods:

"The part which I acted is now to be explained..."

With the letter sealed, my resolve to deliver it to Miss Bennet was as firm as the rising sun. Finding her in the grove near the Parsonage, I approached with a heart full of hope and trepidation. Our encounter was brief; the solemnity of the moment was palpable. Placing the letter into her hands felt akin to setting forth a piece of my very soul adrift, vulnerable to her judgment.

The hours that followed were a testament to my restless state. Colonel Fitzwilliam and I prepared for our departure from both Hunsford and Rosings—a retreat from the battlefield of my own folly. My aunt, Lady Catherine, bid us farewell with her usual mix of imperiousness and indifference to any sentimentality.

The journey from Hunsford was one of quiet introspection. The Colonel, sensing my disquiet, offered no prying questions, for which I was grateful. Our conversation was sparse, limited to the necessary exchanges of travel. My thoughts were consumed by Elizabeth—her face as I left her, the emotions that had danced across her features, and the hope that my words on paper might, in some way, mend the rift between us.

The letter I left in her hands was the most vulnerable act I had ever committed to. It was both an admission of my own failings and a plea for her understanding. Whether it would change her opinion of me, I dared not speculate. I had laid my character before her, and now all was left to the mercy of her judgment.

As the landscape of Kent gave way to the familiar roads leading home, I could not shake the feeling that I was leaving behind a piece of my heart. The Elizabeth I knew would read my letter with a critical eye, but I hoped she would also see the man behind the words—a man who, despite his pride and his errors, was capable of deep feeling and sincerity.

The days ahead will be filled with the business of Pemberley and the demands of my station, but my thoughts will remain with Elizabeth. In the quiet moments, I will wonder if she reads my letter, what she thinks, and whether the truths it contains will soften her opinion of me. Until I have some indication of her feelings, I will carry on, a man touched by love and transformed by the humility that true affection demands.

Fitzwilliam Darcy

May 15, 1812

The bustling streets of London are behind me now as I traverse the well-worn path back to Pemberley. My time in the city was consumed by business—transactions and negotiations that ordinarily would command my full attention. Yet, throughout it all, my thoughts were persistently drawn to a certain Miss Elizabeth Bennet, whose image haunts me still, despite the passing weeks since our last, most tumultuous encounter.

I have been informed that she has returned to her family's estate in Hertfordshire. The news brought an unexpected sense of relief, though it is coupled with a strange emptiness, knowing she is once again beyond my reach. The letter I entrusted to her hands in Kent, the raw exposition of my heart and a detailing of my actions, remains without reply. In the stillness of the night, I wonder if it has altered her perceptions, if the disdain she held for me might be tempered by the truths I revealed.

The city's smog and clamour have given way to the fresh, verdant scents of the countryside, as the carriage rolls ever closer to the sanctuary of Pemberley. My heart longs for the familiar embrace of its grounds, the peaceful respite it offers. I am eager to see my sister Georgiana, whose innocence and warmth are the light of my life. Her letters speak of excitement for our impending guests, yet I detect an undercurrent of anxiety, a shadow that the Wickham affair still casts upon her. I am determined to be the brother she needs, to protect and support her as we face the future together.

Mr. Bingley and his sisters are to join us shortly at Pemberley. The thought of his arrival brings to mind the unresolved matters between him and Miss Jane Bennet, Elizabeth's beloved sister. My role in their separation weighs heavily upon me, and I am resolved to rectify the situation, to pave the way for Bingley's happiness, should his heart still be inclined. This is a debt I owe, not only to my friend but to Elizabeth as well.

As the carriage winds its way through the familiar lanes leading to Pemberley, the estate finally comes into view—a majestic sight that never fails to stir something deep within me. It is more than a home; it is a testament to the Darcy legacy, a legacy I am charged with upholding.

Yet, as I step through its grand entrance, the opulence that surrounds me feels hollow. The absence of Elizabeth's presence is a silent echo in the marble halls, a reminder of what is missing from the grandeur that surrounds me.

In the quiet of my study, surrounded by the portraits of Darcys past, I pen these words with a heavy heart. My sister's joy upon my return was a welcome respite, her embrace a reminder of the love that remains steadfast in my life. But as I prepare to welcome Bingley and his sisters, there is an ache for a different reunion—one that may never come to pass.

The weeks ahead will be filled with the laughter of guests and the warmth of family, but as I look out upon the verdant expanse of Pemberley's grounds, I cannot help but wish that Elizabeth could share in this beauty. That she might walk these gardens and halls, her hand clasped in mine, her eyes alight with the wonder I long to show her.

For now, I must content myself with the duties of a host and the companionship of my sister. I will welcome my friends with open arms and, perhaps, in the joy of their company, find a momentary respite from the yearning that has taken root in my heart.

Fitzwilliam Darcy

May 16, 1812

Today, the tranquility of Pemberley was broken by the most startling of occurrences, one that has left my mind in a state of turmoil and my heart racing with an emotion I had not anticipated to feel so acutely again. It was an encounter that unfolded so unexpectedly that I am still grappling to comprehend its significance.

The morning had dawned with a clear blue sky, and the sun's rays cast a golden glow upon the lush grounds of my ancestral home. I had ventured out for a solitary walk to clear my mind, as the anticipation of Bingley's arrival, along with his sisters, weighed heavily upon me. Not to mention the eagerness with which I awaited Georgiana's presence, her letters having been my only solace since my departure from Kent.

As I walked across the lawn towards the river, lost in thought, the last person I expected to see was Elizabeth Bennet. Yet there she was, her back to me as she admired the house with her uncle and aunt. I could not fathom the purpose of her visit, nor could I retreat without notice. Our eyes met, and in that moment, a rush of emotions overcame me—the memory of our last parting, the letter I had written, and the silence that followed.

We were within mere yards of each other when she turned and saw me. The blush that rose to her cheeks mirrored my own as a startling warmth spread through me. She appeared taken aback, and I, too, was momentarily frozen in place by the sight of her.

Recovering my composure, I approached her party. My voice, when I greeted her, lacked its usual steadiness, revealing the inner conflict I felt. Her response was polite, but her eyes held a wariness that pained me. I inquired after her family with as much civility as I could muster, all the while conscious of the impropriety of her finding me here, and I, her.

Our conversation was a dance of awkward silences and hesitant words. The inquiries I made regarding her stay in Derbyshire and her departure from Longbourn were repeated more often than decorum would dictate. It was clear that we were both equally affected, our minds preoccupied with thoughts that rendered speech difficult.

Upon their introduction, I found Miss Bennet's relatives to be people of amiable character and respectable appearance—a far cry from the lack of propriety I had perceived in some of her other connections. Her aunt and uncle, the Gardiners, carried themselves with an ease and civility that spoke well of their sense and breeding. I found Mr. Gardiner to be a gentleman of both intelligence and taste, and I was pleasantly surprised by the genuine warmth and the absence of pretension in their demeanor.

My offer to Mr. Gardiner of the fishing in my streams was a gesture of goodwill I hoped would be received without obligation, and I believe it was taken as such. It afforded me a quiet satisfaction to extend this courtesy, and I was gratified to see it accepted with genuine appreciation by both Mr. Gardiner and his wife. Their admiration of Pemberley's beauty was flattering, and Mrs. Gardiner's praise, in particular, was delivered with an enthusiasm that, under different circumstances, might have brought a smile to my face.

The idea that Miss Bennet should meet Georgiana is one that has occupied my thoughts more than I care to admit. The prospect of introducing the two most esteemed ladies in my life to one another is both thrilling and daunting in equal measure. My sister, with her gentle nature and kindness of heart, has long been my joy and concern. I have watched her recover from the ordeal with Wickham—a recovery made all the more remarkable by the strength of her character and the sweetness of her disposition.

I am keenly aware of the beneficial influence Elizabeth might have upon Georgiana, and the thought that the two might form a friendship fills me with an eager anticipation. Yet, I cannot ignore the flutter of anxiety at how such an introduction might be perceived by Elizabeth, or how it may affect her view of me.

As I reflect on this day's encounter and the consequent emotions it has evoked, I cannot help but feel that my invitation to Elizabeth was more than a mere formality. There is a part of me—a part I can scarcely acknowledge—that hopes for her acceptance not just for the sake of propriety, but from a desire to be near her once more, to see her interact with Georgiana, and to perhaps share in the harmony and peace that Pemberley brings to all who visit.

Yet, I must guard against such expectations. The past cannot be so easily forgotten, and the wounds I have inflicted upon her heart may yet be too fresh for such an acquaintance to be anything but a source of discomfort for her. Still, the hope remains—an ember that refuses to be extinguished—that she might come to see the man I truly am, and the home that could have been hers..

I watched her walk away, every instinct urging me to call her back, to speak openly of the feelings that coursed through me, yet I remained still. What could I say that had not been said in my letter? What could I offer her now, after all that had transpired?

I returned to the house, my mind a tumult of hope and despair. The sight of Elizabeth at Pemberley, the place I hold most dear, stirred within me a longing that I had tried to bury. It was as though her presence here was a sign, a whisper of fate that perhaps all was not lost between us.

Yet, I am reminded of the divide that stands firm—her opinion of me, though perhaps softened, is still tainted by the past. How can I hope for her affection when I have caused her such pain?

As I sit here in my study, the image of Elizabeth walking through the grounds of Pemberley is etched into my mind. It is both a torment and a comfort, a reminder of what could be if the shadows of our past could be dispelled.

Tomorrow, I will see my sister again, and soon, Bingley and his party will arrive. I must prepare to greet them with the hospitality that befits the master of Pemberley. Yet, in the quiet moments, amidst the laughter and conversation, I know my thoughts will stray to the woman who has unwittingly captured the entirety of my heart.

Fitzwilliam Darcy

May 20, 1812

The anticipation that filled me last evening was unlike any I have experienced before. It was not the familiar thrill of hosting a distinguished party at Pemberley, nor was it solely the joy of being reunited with dear Georgiana. It was the knowledge that today would bring Elizabeth into my home once more, this time as my invited guest.

As I awoke this morning, the manor was already astir with preparations. The knowledge of the Gardiners' and Elizabeth's impending visit injected an unusual energy into the household. Servants moved with a purpose, and an air of expectancy settled over Pemberley like a fine mist upon the moors at dawn.

I found myself pacing the gallery, glancing occasionally through the tall windows overlooking the drive, my gaze seeking the first signs of their carriage. The very notion that Elizabeth would soon be walking through the halls of my ancestral home, halls I had once hoped might become as familiar to her as they are to me, was both exhilarating and disquieting.

The sound of wheels on the gravel finally drew my attention, and I watched as the carriage that bore Elizabeth and her relatives approached. My heart quickened, and I felt an uncharacteristic nervousness grip me. It was a sensation that no amount of social standing or wealth could shield me from—the raw, unguarded feeling of a man on the cusp of seeing the woman who had unwittingly taken possession of his heart.

As they alighted from the carriage, I saw Elizabeth's face, alight with what I hoped was pleasure but also marked by the unmistakable signs of apprehension. Her uncle and aunt, the Gardiners, carried themselves with an ease that belied their surprise at the grandeur of Pemberley. I greeted them with as much warmth and civility as I could muster, conscious of their importance to Elizabeth and desiring earnestly to make a favorable impression.

Introducing Georgiana to Elizabeth was a moment of profound significance. I observed them both with an intensity that bordered on the paternal. Georgiana, my sweet sister, bore a shyness that was often mistaken for pride, much like myself. Elizabeth's grace in engaging her in conversation, drawing her out with gentle questions and an attentive ear, filled me with a gratitude that was as deep as the Derbyshire valleys.

As Bingley joined our small gathering, his cheerfulness and unaffected cordiality served to lighten the atmosphere. I could discern no trace of resentment in Elizabeth's manner towards him, a testament to her forgiving nature and generous spirit. It was evident that Bingley still held her sister Jane in high regard, and I watched as he sought out information about the Bennet family with a keen interest that spoke volumes.

In the presence of Elizabeth and her relations, I found myself striving to be the very best version of myself. The hauteur and reserve that had once been my armor in society fell away, leaving a man eager to be seen as deserving of their good opinion. I was attentive to Mr. Gardiner's interest in fishing, offering whatever assistance and access he might desire during his stay.

Throughout the visit, my eyes would find their way back to Elizabeth, seeking her approval or a sign of encouragement. The change in my own behavior was not lost on me; where once I would have sought to impress with grandeur and consequence, now I sought to connect with sincerity and kindness.

As the afternoon wore on and the time for their departure drew near, I felt a reluctance to see them go. The invitation for them to dine at Pemberley was extended with an earnestness that surprised even me. It was an invitation borne out of a desire to extend this pleasant interlude, to bask a while longer in the light of Elizabeth's presence.

As they left, I escorted them to their carriage, my mind already racing with the thought of our next meeting. In the quiet that followed their departure, I felt an uncharacteristic sense of hopefulness. The walls of Pemberley seemed to whisper with the possibility of a future I had scarcely allowed myself to dream of—one that might, just might, include Elizabeth by my side.

Fitzwilliam Darcy

May 24, 1812

It is a truth universally acknowledged that the master of Pemberley must be in want of a companion. As the morning sun peeked through the curtains of my bedchamber, that sentiment, once a source of mild amusement, now weighed heavily upon my heart. Today, Elizabeth, alongside her esteemed relatives, the Gardiners, were to visit. My mind was awash with the hope and trepidation of a schoolboy rather than the composed master of a grand estate.

Upon their arrival, they were shown into the saloon—a room of cool, northern aspect, where the summer's light danced upon the oaken floor. There, amidst the grandeur of Pemberley, Miss Darcy received our guests with a civility that belied her inner turmoil. The poor girl's shyness, I fear, oft gives the unfortunate impression of aloofness, which could not be further from the truth of her gentle nature.

Mrs. Hurst and Miss Bingley offered their greetings with a perfunctory air, their courtesies falling just shy of genuine warmth. It was Mrs. Annesley who rose to the occasion, her genteel manners and agreeable conversation bridging the gap left by the others' reticence. With her aid, Mrs. Gardiner and, at intervals, Elizabeth herself kept the discourse flowing, much to my sister's relief, who ventured only the briefest of sentences amidst the fear of committing some social misstep.

I was absent when they first arrived, detained by the estate's affairs. Upon entering the saloon, I was met with a tableau that set my heart racing: Elizabeth, resplendent in her simplicity, stood conversing with my sister and Mrs. Annesley, her poise and grace underscoring the awkwardness of the others.

The conversation naturally fell to me to sustain, and I made mention to Elizabeth, "They will join me early to-morrow," referring to Bingley and my sisters, "and among them are some who will claim an acquaintance with you—Mr. Bingley and his sisters."

Her response was a modest bow, her attention flitting between myself and Miss Bingley, who observed us with a scrutiny I found most displeasing.

It was not long before Bingley himself made his entrance. His easy demeanor and unaffected cordiality were a breath of fresh air, his inquiries after her family both friendly and general. To my satisfaction, Elizabeth's response was polite and equally unreserved, a testament to her forgiving disposition.

As we engaged in conversation, I found myself acutely aware of Elizabeth's every glance, every gesture, her presence commanding my attention in a manner I could scarcely control. The room was alive with the undercurrents of unspoken thoughts and subtle glances, the connection between Bingley and Elizabeth palpable even as they spoke of trivial matters.

Miss Bingley's civility did not last; her remarks thinly concealed the jealousy and spite that I knew all too well. "Pray, Miss Eliza, are not the ——shire militia removed from Meryton? They must be a great loss to your family," she said with a sneer that did not escape my notice, nor the distress it caused Elizabeth.

I saw the color rise to Elizabeth's cheeks, her composure briefly faltering under the weight of the insinuation. Yet, she replied with a steadiness that filled me with admiration: "They are removed into ——shire, I believe." Her voice was even, though the implication behind Miss Bingley's words was clear to us both.

In due course, refreshments were served, and the party congregated around the table, the variety of fruits providing a welcome distraction from the tension. I took the opportunity to speak with Elizabeth, to express my genuine desire for her and her relatives to join us for dinner at Pemberley. It was an invitation offered from the deepest reaches of my heart, a chance to share with her the hospitality of my home.

The visit, though brief, was a revelation. As they departed, I was left with a sense of satisfaction and longing. The image of Elizabeth at Pemberley, so natural and yet so profound, lingered in my mind.

In the privacy of my study, I reflected on the events of the morning. The sight of Elizabeth engaged in conversation with Georgiana, the subtle interplay of looks and words—all served to solidify my resolve. She must know the depth of my affection, the sincerity of my intentions. My hope was that the forthcoming dinner would provide an opportunity to further demonstrate my esteem for her.

Yet, as the day drew to a close and I prepared for the evening, I could not shake the feeling that Elizabeth's visit to Pemberley was a turning point, a moment in time that might herald the beginning of a new chapter in our acquaintance—one that I fervently wished would lead to a more intimate connection.

Fitzwilliam Darcy

August 2, 1812

The serene halls of Pemberley, once a haven of peace and reflection, today bore witness to a scene of such distress that even now, as I commit these events to paper, my hand trembles with the agitation of the memory.

Elizabeth, ashen-faced and trembling, had just been conveyed the most grievous news from Longbourn. The servant had scarcely left the room, his hurried footsteps echoing through the corridor, as I stood, perplexed and alarmed, by her side. Her posture spoke of a fragility and despair so profound that it pierced through the very armor of my composure.

"Good God! what is the matter?" I cried, my words a mixture of concern and a lack of decorum I could not then afford to consider. Seeing her so distressed, I felt my own heart clench in a vice of empathy. "I will not detain you a minute; but let me, or let the servant, go after Mr. and Mrs. Gardiner. You are not well enough; you cannot go yourself."

Elizabeth, my dear Elizabeth, was indeed in no state to venture out. Her knees betrayed her strength, and her voice, when she spoke, was but a whisper of its former self. It pained me to see her thus, to witness the usually spirited and lively woman I had come to admire so deeply reduced to such helplessness.

When she managed to convey the nature of her distress—that her youngest sister Lydia had eloped, thrown herself into the power of that scoundrel Wickham—I felt as though the ground had shifted beneath me. My astonishment was complete, and a silent curse on Wickham's name went unvoiced, for the sake of the lady before me.

Elizabeth's tears were a sight I shall never forget—tears of shame, of regret, and of a profound sorrow that resonated through the very core of my being. "It cannot be concealed from anyone. My youngest sister has left all her friends—has eloped; has thrown herself into the power of—of Mr. Wickham. They are gone off together from Brighton. You know him too well to doubt the rest. She has no money, no connections, nothing that can tempt him to—she is lost for ever."

The words cut through me, not only for the pain they caused Elizabeth but for the role I had unwittingly played in this tragedy. Had I but revealed Wickham's true character to the world, could this disaster have been averted? The guilt was a bitter draft, and I partook of it fully as I stood there, helpless to offer any solace to the woman whose world had come crashing down around her.

The subsequent conversation was a blur of distress and commiseration. I asked after the efforts made to recover Lydia, shared in the grim assessment of the situation, and felt keenly the frustration and futility of the moment. Elizabeth's lament—that she might have prevented this calamity had she only shared what she knew of Wickham—echoed my own internal reproach.

As propriety dictated, I offered to leave, to summon her maid, to do anything that might alleviate her immediate suffering, yet my heart screamed to stay, to wrap her in the security of my arms and to vow to make this right. But I was a gentleman, and her honor and well-being were paramount.

"I am grieved, indeed," was all I could utter, the words hollow against the gravity of her pain. "Grieved—shocked. But is it certain, absolutely certain?"

The confirmation of the elopement, the futile search, and the lack of hope for a happy resolution were like a dirge to my soul. Yet, as I made my leave, promising discretion and expressing my deepest regrets, I knew that this could not be the end. I would not allow it.

It was a somber reflection that followed their hasty departure—a reflection on the nature of love, of family, and of honor. The image of Elizabeth, so distraught and so alone, was seared into my mind, and I resolved then and there that I would take up the mantle of this burden.

I would find Lydia and Wickham, and I would do everything within my power to restore the Bennet family's good name, for Elizabeth's sake, and for the sake of the affection I held for her, which, even now, refused to be extinguished.

The journey ahead would be fraught with difficulty and uncertainty, but as I set out from Pemberley, I was driven by a newfound purpose and a determination that would not waver. For Elizabeth, for her family, and for the future that I still dared to hope might be ours, I would face this challenge with all the resolve of a man fighting for the very essence of his soul.

Fitzwilliam Darcy

August 3, 1812

As my carriage rolls steadily towards London, the rhythm of the wheels upon the road is a constant reminder of the urgency that propels me forth. The countryside, typically a source of contemplative solace, now passes by in a blur—each mile traversed a step closer to the resolution of a matter most distressing.

The gravity of the situation is not lost upon me. Lydia Bennet's elopement with that scoundrel, Wickham, has cast a shadow over the lives of those I have come to hold in high regard. The memory of Elizabeth's countenance—pale and distraught as she conveyed the dire news—lingers in my mind, igniting a determination that borders on the ferocious.

Elizabeth's subsequent expression of regret—that she had not shared her knowledge of Wickham's true nature with her family—echoed my own self-reproach. "I am grieved, indeed," was all I could manage, my words a paltry offering in the face of her anguish. "Grieved—shocked. But is it certain, absolutely certain?"

The confirmation did little to ease the dread that had taken root within my chest. With each detail she provided, the path before me became clearer. My resolve to correct this wrong, to restore the

Bennets' honor and to bring Lydia back from the precipice of ruin, solidified into a vow as unyielding as the steel of a well-forged blade.

As I bid Elizabeth farewell, promising discretion and expressing my sincerest wishes for a resolution, I knew that the matter would not end with mere words of sympathy. I must act, and with a swiftness that allows no room for hesitation or delay.

Now, ensconced within my carriage, I find myself replaying the events of the morning—Elizabeth's distress, her family's plight, and my own role in this sordid affair. There is a fervor in my breast, a passion to set things right that goes beyond duty or honor. It is born of a love that I have attempted to deny, to suppress, but which now fuels my every action.

My thoughts turn to Elizabeth, and I am beset by a melange of emotions. Admiration, regret, longing, and an affection that has grown in depth and fervency with each passing moment we have shared. I am determined not only to rectify the wrongs done by Wickham but also to prove myself worthy of her esteem, to demonstrate through my deeds the sincerity of my feelings.

The road to London stretches out before me, a tangible representation of the journey upon which I am embarked. It is a path fraught with uncertainty, but I am undeterred. For Elizabeth, for the Bennet family, and for the future happiness that I dare still hope for, I will face whatever trials may come.

The carriage continues on, and with it, my resolve grows ever stronger. Wickham will be found, and Lydia will be returned to her family. Of this, I am determined. There can be no other outcome, for I am driven by an ardor that will accept nothing less than success.

Fitzwilliam Darcy

August 10, 1812

The labyrinthine streets of London, with their ceaseless din and murky shadows, are a far cry from the pastoral tranquility of Pemberley. In this sprawling metropolis where fortunes are made and lost, where every sort of character roams, I find myself on a quest that seems both noble and ignoble—for I am here to negotiate with a scoundrel.

The pursuit of Wickham and Lydia has led me to the less reputable corners of the city, places where the genteel seldom venture. Yet venture I must, for the stakes are higher than mere reputation. In the days since I left Elizabeth, her tearful countenance has been my constant companion, a silent reproach for my past inaction and a spur to rectify the present calamity.

Through a network of acquaintances and the employment of considerable resources, I have located the wretched pair. Wickham, ever the charming rogue, was found in a gaming house, and Lydia, I regret to say, was in a state unbefitting a lady of her station. The sight of her—so young, so carefree, yet so perilously close to ruin—struck a chord within me. In her, I saw the potential downfall of Elizabeth's family, the blemish that could mar their good name irreparably.

With a firmness born of necessity, I arranged for their immediate removal to a more appropriate lodging. The negotiations with Wickham were as sordid as the man himself. His debts, as I had anticipated, were numerous and pressing. He had no intention of marrying Lydia, no thoughts for her welfare, only for his own skin and means. It was a display of character so vile that it tested the very limits of my restraint.

Yet, for the sake of Elizabeth and her family, I concealed my revulsion and proceeded with the bargaining. It was agreed that I would settle his most pressing debts and provide a modest income, in return for his marrying Lydia. The sum involved was not insignificant, but there was no price too high for Elizabeth's peace of mind.

The matter of the wedding was arranged with haste, the ceremony to be conducted with a discretion that would, I hoped, preserve what little dignity remained for the Bennet family. As for Lydia, I took it upon myself to escort her to the Gardiners' residence, where the gravity of her actions would no doubt be made clear to her.

Upon seeing the Gardiners, I was struck by the blend of relief and concern that marked their countenances. They were Elizabeth's kin, and in them, I saw reflected her own virtues of kindness and fortitude.

"I have come to make amends," I began, my voice betraying none of the turmoil that churned within. "The fault is mine. I should have made the character of that man known to the world. He has deceived, used, and abandoned young women before, and he shall not do so again. I will see to it that he marries Lydia."

Mr. Gardiner, a man of sense and feeling, protested. "You cannot hold yourself responsible for Wickham's actions, Mr. Darcy. It is he who has wronged us, not you."

But I was resolute. "I cannot undo what has been done, but I can mitigate the damage. I will ensure their marriage, and I will bear the costs of the wedding and Wickham's debts. It is the least I can do."

Mrs. Gardiner's eyes met mine, a silent understanding passing between us. In her gaze, I saw Elizabeth's own compassion, her own strength. "This is a generous offer, Mr. Darcy," she said softly. "We are in your debt."

"No," I replied firmly, "there will be no talk of debts between us. This is my doing, and I will see it through to the end."

As I left the Gardiners' home, the weight of my undertaking settled upon me with a gravity that was both burdensome and liberating. In seeking to restore Lydia's honor, I found a deeper resolve within myself—a resolve to be the man worthy of Elizabeth's love, to be her protector, her advocate, her unwavering ally.

Before me lies a path fraught with challenges, but I am determined to walk it, to do what honor and affection demand. For Elizabeth, for her family, and for the future that I hope might yet be ours, no obstacle shall be insurmountable.

Fitzwilliam Darcy

August 15, 1812

The morning dawned not with the clear, bright promise to which I am accustomed at Pemberley, but with a London shrouded in a fog that seemed to reflect the somber task at hand. Today, I am to witness the union of Mr. George Wickham and Miss Lydia Bennet—a wedding that is the result of necessity rather than romance, of scandal rather than joy.

The church, a modest edifice tucked away in a quiet corner of the city, was chosen for its discretion. The air within was cool and still, and as I entered, the last remnants of incense from morning prayers lingered, a ghostly presence. The pews stood empty, save for a few necessary witnesses. There would be no grand celebration here, no pealing of bells to announce the joyous event. The very atmosphere was charged with an unspoken understanding of the gravity and reluctance that brought us to this juncture.

Wickham, ever the charmer, wore an expression of nonchalance that belied the severity of his situation. He greeted me with that same easy smile I had once considered the mark of friendship, a smile I now knew to be as false as the man himself. Beside him stood Lydia, whose youthful exuberance appeared undiminished by the scandal she had wrought. The sight of her, so blithely unaware of the precipice upon which she teetered, caused within me a profound sadness.

I took my place, a silent guardian of propriety, ensuring that the ceremony proceeded as agreed. The vows were exchanged with a hollowness that echoed off the stone walls, and as the couple spoke the sacred words, I could not help but ponder the irony of it all. What should have been a sacred covenant was, in this case, little more than a transaction—a means to secure a semblance of respectability for a young woman who scarcely understood its value.

As the clergyman pronounced them husband and wife, I felt a peculiar tightness in my chest—not for the fate of Wickham, who was beyond my concern, but for Lydia and the family she had so carelessly imperiled. I thought of Elizabeth, of her distress and her dignity in the face of such adversity, and it steeled my resolve.

The ceremony concluded with perfunctory efficiency, and the newlyweds emerged into the pale light of day. Wickham's debts would be settled, his commission purchased, and in return, he would carry the name of Bennet into the murky waters of his existence. It was a heavy price, but one I paid willingly for the peace it might bring to Elizabeth and her family.

As I watched the carriage bearing the Wickhams away from the church, a wave of relief washed over me, tempered by the knowledge that the true work of mending the Bennets' fractured peace was only just beginning. In the days to come, I would endeavor to ensure that Lydia's indiscretion would not taint the prospects of her sisters, nor cast a shadow upon their respectable standing in society.

Retreating from the church, I felt the weight of the day's events settle upon me. Yet amid the tumult of emotions, there was also a clarity of purpose. Elizabeth, her approbation, and the chance to earn her esteem, were now the lodestars by which I would navigate.

As I returned to my carriage, the London fog seemed to lift slightly, a metaphor, perhaps, for the clearing of the path before me. The road to redemption—for Lydia, for the Bennets, and for myself—would be long and fraught with challenges. But I was ready to walk it with a steadfast heart and an unwavering commitment to the woman who had come to mean more to me than I had ever thought possible.

Fitzwilliam Darcy

August 24, 1812

The matter of Wickham and Lydia being settled, albeit in a manner far from the joyous unions of which poets sing, I find myself on a journey of a decidedly different nature. The road from London to Netherfield Park is one I have traveled before, yet today it is as if I traverse a different path altogether—a path of humility and contrition.

My carriage rolls through the countryside, the sun dappled fields a stark contrast to the somber reflections that occupy my thoughts. It is a journey not of mere miles, but of the soul. I am to meet with my friend Bingley, to lay bare a truth I have concealed, and in doing so, to right a wrong that has lain heavy upon my conscience.

Bingley greets me with his usual affability, yet I detect a shadow of confusion in his eyes, a question unspoken. I do not delay, for the hour is ripe and my resolve firm.

"Charles," I begin, my voice steady despite the tumult within, "I have come to speak of a matter most grave, one which concerns your heart and the happiness of a lady most dear to us both."

He looks at me, his brow furrowed in concern, and urges me to continue.

"It is of Miss Jane Bennet I wish to speak," I say, and the very mention of her name seems to strike him, an arrow to the heart. "In my misguided judgment, I concealed from you her presence in London, believing it to be in your best interest. I see now that I erred, that I did you both a disservice."

Bingley is silent, the weight of my confession hanging between us like the morning mist.

"You saw her affection for me as mere politeness," he says, the hurt evident in his voice.

"I did," I admit, "and for that, I am truly sorry. I was wrong, Bingley. Miss Bennet's regard for you is genuine, and I have come to give not only my apologies but my blessing, should you still be inclined to seek her hand."

His astonishment is palpable, a mixture of relief and disbelief. "You mean..."

"Yes," I affirm, "I have seen the depth of her affection for you, the pain your separation has caused. If you would still have her, I would see you both happily united."

The joy that alights upon Bingley's face is a balm to my soul. He clasps my hand, his gratitude heartfelt and sincere.

"Darcy, I cannot thank you enough," he says. "You have given me back my hope."

We speak at length, of love and of the trials that test it. I reveal to him all that I have learned, all that I have come to understand about the matters of the heart. And as we converse, a plan is formed—a return to Longbourn, where Bingley might once again pursue the affections of Miss Bennet with my full support.

The journey to Longbourn is one of cautious optimism. Bingley is abuzz with nervous energy, the prospect of seeing Jane again reigniting the flame that had never truly been extinguished. I, too, am not immune to the anticipation that such a journey entails, for it brings me closer to Elizabeth, to the possibility of reconciliation and, dare I hope, a future shared.

We arrive at Netherfield under the pretense of a casual visit, but our true intentions are far from casual. Bingley wastes no time, his eagerness to see Jane driving him forward. I accompany him, a silent ally in his quest for happiness.

The sight of Longbourn in the distance stirs within me a myriad of emotions. It is here that I first laid eyes upon Elizabeth, here that I first battled with the pride and prejudice that have since shaped my destiny.

As the carriage draws to a stop, I steel myself for the encounter to come. My own affections, though carefully guarded, have not waned. I am resolved to face whatever reception awaits me, for the sake of my friend and for the sake of the woman who has unwittingly claimed my heart.

Fitzwilliam Darcy

September 1, 1812

As the carriage drew near to the familiar estate of Longbourn, a sense of profound trepidation settled within me. The curtains of foliage parted to reveal the Bennet family home, a sight which once brought a mixture of disdain and indifference, now stirred a deep and complex well of emotions—a testament to the indelible mark Elizabeth has left upon me.

The visit today was ostensibly for Bingley to renew his attentions to the fair Jane, yet my own heart harbored its hidden agenda, a hope for a glimpse of Elizabeth and a chance to gauge the tenor of her feelings towards me since the unfortunate revelations at Pemberley.

Upon our arrival, it was evident that the household was astir with a flurry of activity. The presence of two eligible gentlemen was no small event in such a country abode, and I felt the weight of many eyes upon us as we were shown into the parlor.

Jane, the ever-graceful elder Bennet sister, received us with a composure that belied the paleness of her cheeks. Her serene countenance was a balm to Bingley's evident nerves, and as I beheld them, the rightness of their union seemed as clear as day.

Elizabeth, however, was another matter altogether. She sat, her fingers diligently working at her embroidery, a picture of focused composure. Yet as we entered, I saw her hands still, an unspoken tension gripping her. She dared only a single glance in my direction—a glance that carried with it the weight of our shared past and the uncertainty of our future.

Her countenance was one of serious reflection, reminiscent more of our time in Hertfordshire than the ease she exhibited at Pemberley. It pained me to see her so, to feel the barriers that lay between us, walls not of distance but of circumstance and misunderstanding.

Mrs. Bennet, oblivious to the undercurrents, received us with a display of civility that had her daughters cringing. Elizabeth's discomfort was palpable as her mother spoke of Lydia's marriage, boasting of the event while unwittingly casting aspersions upon my character.

The agony of the moment was acute, and I found myself in the regrettable position of having little to say. My inquiries after the Gardiners were met with confusion from Elizabeth, a response that served only to deepen the chasm of our strained civility.

As the visit wore on, I found myself caught between the desire to speak freely with Elizabeth and the constraints of propriety which held us both firmly in their grasp. I yearned to convey all that had transpired, all that I had done in the name of her family's honor, yet the words would not come. Instead, I was reduced to silent observation, to stolen glances that revealed more than I could articulate.

When the opportunity for conversation arose, it was brief and fraught with difficulty. Elizabeth's inquiry after Georgiana was met with a simple affirmation, yet even this small exchange was a connection—a thread of hope that perhaps not all was lost between us.

Mrs. Bennet's conversation turned to the prospect of shooting on Mr. Bennet's land, an invitation extended to Bingley with her usual lack of subtlety. The discomfort of the moment was shared by all, a reminder of the societal dance we were all engaged in, where steps were dictated by expectation and the music played on regardless of the players' readiness.

As we took our leave, the promise of a dinner invitation in the near future was secured. Mrs. Bennet, ever the matchmaker, made plain her intentions, leaving Bingley both pleased and embarrassed by the attention.

The carriage ride back to Netherfield was one of contemplation. Bingley was buoyant with hope, his heart clearly as much Jane's as it ever was. As for myself, I was awash in a sea of introspection. The sight of Elizabeth, her beauty undiminished by the trials she had endured, had rekindled in me all the affection and admiration I had fought so hard to suppress.

In the quiet of my own chambers, I found solace in the written word, pouring my reflections onto these pages. The path that lay before me was unclear, yet one thing remained certain: Elizabeth Bennet had captured my heart, and I was powerless to reclaim it. Whether our story would find a resolution in harmony or heartbreak, only time would tell.

Fitzwilliam Darcy

September 10, 1812

The invitation to dine at Longbourn, once a matter of indifference, now held a significance that could not be overstated. It was to be an evening of consequence, for Bingley and myself, for reasons both public and personal. As our carriage traversed the familiar path, I found myself in a state of introspection, pondering the possible outcomes of the night ahead.

Upon our punctual arrival, the Bennet household was aflutter with activity, the anticipation of the evening palpable in the air. Mrs. Bennet's welcome was effusive in its civility, though her attention was soon diverted by the task of hosting. Jane's reception of Bingley was marked by an unspoken understanding, a look exchanged that seemed to seal his fate.

I, however, turned my gaze towards Elizabeth, whose attempts at calm betrayed her inner turmoil. She sat diligently at her needlework, her fingers moving with a practiced grace that spoke of a desire for distraction. Yet, as I entered, her hands stilled momentarily—a silent testament to the effect of my presence.

The dinner was a lively affair, with conversation flowing as freely as the wine. Jane, the image of tranquility, was seated beside Bingley, who could scarcely contain his admiration for her. Mrs. Bennet's machinations were transparent, yet none could fault the mother for seeking the happiness of her child.

As for Elizabeth and myself, we were seated at a cruel distance, separated not only by the expanse of the table but by an undercurrent of unresolved emotions. Despite my proximity to Mrs. Bennet, a woman of no small opinion, my attention was invariably drawn to

Elizabeth. Her presence was magnetic, her every glance and gesture observed with an intensity I could scarcely conceal.

Throughout the meal, my thoughts were consumed by Elizabeth's well-being and the family's reception of my actions. I longed to convey the depth of my regard for her, to speak of matters left unsaid, yet the presence of her mother rendered such discourse impossible.

As the evening progressed, the hope for a moment of private conversation with Elizabeth grew. With each passing minute, I felt the weight of expectation, the desire to bridge the gap between us. Yet, as the gentlemen adjourned to the drawing-room, I found myself thwarted by the throng of ladies and the strategic positioning of the Bennet sisters.

Elizabeth's whisper to me, though brief, was a balm to my restless spirit. "Is your sister at Pemberley still?" she inquired, a question that betrayed her continued interest in my world.

"Yes; she will remain there till Christmas," I replied, seizing the opportunity to converse, however briefly.

"And quite alone? Have all her friends left her?" Her voice was laced with genuine concern, a concern I shared for Georgiana's well-being.

"Mrs. Annesley is with her," I assured her. "The others have been gone on to Scarborough these three weeks."

Our exchange was cut short by the commotion of the room, and I was soon ensnared by Mrs. Bennet's call for whist players. As the card tables were arranged, I felt a keen sense of loss, my evening's enjoyment sacrificed upon the altar of social obligation.

Seated at the whist table, my mind was only partially on the game; my thoughts wandered incessantly to Elizabeth. I could sense her frustration from across the room, her own displeasure at the evening's turn of events. And yet, despite the distance, I found myself attempting to catch her eye, to communicate through silent glances that which could not be spoken aloud.

The evening waned, and with it, my hopes of meaningful discourse with Elizabeth. The games of cards and conversation continued, a dance of social niceties that masked the true desires of the heart. It was an evening of missed opportunities, of words unspoken and feelings unexpressed.

As I retired to my room at Netherfield later that night, the quiet of the night was a stark contrast to the bustle of Longbourn. The events of the evening replayed in my mind, a litany of what might have been. Yet, amidst the disappointment, there remained a hope that a future encounter might yield a different result.

For now, I must be content with the knowledge that my affection for Elizabeth Bennet remains undiminished, a sentiment I hold in secret, waiting for the moment when it can be declared openly and without reservation.

Fitzwilliam Darcy

September 20, 1812

The morning dew still clung to the grass as I prepared for my departure to London. Although this venture is for business, it is intertwined with matters of the heart and the happiness of those dear to me. My carriage awaits, and as I step into it, my mind reflects on the recent events at Netherfield and the future that now seems brighter for my dear friend Bingley.

My intent is to return to Netherfield in a ten-day's time, but first, I must attend to various affairs that require my attention in the city. It is a time of careful planning and execution, for the happiness of my sister Georgiana and Bingley's newfound joy are now closely connected to my own endeavors.

As the landscape passes by my window, my thoughts turn to the news I am to share with Georgiana. The engagement of Charles Bingley to Jane Bennet is a matter of great joy, one which I wholeheartedly endorse. It is an alliance that not only brings together two deserving souls but also signifies a new chapter for our intertwined families.

The thought of Bingley's contented future brings a smile to my lips. His unwavering affection for Jane has finally been allowed to flourish, and I take pride in having played a part in removing the obstacles that once stood in their way. His happiness is as important to me as my own, and I foresee many pleasant gatherings in the years to come.

As for Georgiana, the news will be received with equal parts surprise and delight. Her fondness for Jane is genuine, and the prospect of welcoming her as a sister will be a source of great happiness. I anticipate our reunion with eagerness, for I have much to discuss with her, not least of which is the role she may play in the upcoming nuptials.

London approaches, its skyline a familiar silhouette against the morning sky. The city is a hub of activity and commerce, a stark contrast to the pastoral calm of the countryside I have left behind. Yet, amidst the hustle and bustle, there is a tranquility in my heart—a tranquility born of the knowledge that love and friendship have triumphed.

My stay in London will be brief, but necessary. The matters at hand are pressing, and I am determined to see them settled with efficiency and care. My solicitors await, and I am ready to delve into the world of ledgers and legalities, ensuring that all is in order for my swift return to Netherfield and the joyous events that are to follow.

As I step out of the carriage and into the thrum of London life, I carry with me the knowledge that the days ahead hold promise and celebration. The union of Bingley and Jane is but the beginning of a series of joyful occasions, and I am honored to be a part of them.

And what of Elizabeth, I wonder? Her image lingers in my mind—a beacon guiding me through the fog of uncertainty. Her future, and perhaps our shared destiny, remain questions yet unanswered. But for now, I must focus on the tasks before me, confident that time will reveal all in due course.

Fitzwilliam Darcy

October 2, 1812

Today, I write under the most extraordinary and unforeseen circumstances, having been visited by none other than my aunt, Lady Catherine de Bourgh. Her abrupt arrival in London was as unexpected as the tempestuous news she carried with her—a news that pertains directly to my deepest desires and the subject of my heart's consternation, Miss Elizabeth Bennet.

Lady Catherine's countenance was stormy as she swept into my study, her temperament as agitated as the winds that buffeted the windows of Darcy House. With little regard for the usual pleasantries, she launched into a recitation of her recent actions, ones which have left me both aghast and secretly elated.

She recounted, with a mixture of indignation and disbelief, a visit she had made to Longbourn, the home of the Bennets. Her purpose, as she unabashedly confessed, was to confront Miss Elizabeth about the rumors that had reached her ears—rumors of an impending engagement between myself and the youngest Miss Bennet.

My pulse quickened at the mention of Elizabeth's name, and I listened intently as Lady Catherine described the encounter. Her narrative was laced with the arrogance and condescension I have come to expect from her, but it was the reaction of Elizabeth that held me captive.

According to my aunt, she had demanded from Elizabeth a renunciation of any engagement to me, an assurance that no such understanding existed or would ever be formed. Elizabeth, with a spirit and steadiness that could only command my deepest respect and admiration, refused to be swayed by Lady Catherine's imperious demands.

"She would not give her promise!" Lady Catherine exclaimed, her voice rising in incredulity. "The impertinence of the girl! I told her in no uncertain terms the impropriety of such a match, the disparity in rank and fortune! Yet, she held her ground, insisting that she was not to be intimidated into any submission!"

I masked my reaction from Lady Catherine, maintaining a composure that belied the tumult within me. To hear of Elizabeth's defiance, her refusal to deny the possibility of an attachment between us, stirred a hope I had scarcely dared to entertain.

The encounter had ended with no concession from Elizabeth, and Lady Catherine had left Longbourn in a state of heightened exasperation, determined to seek my assurances that I would not disgrace the family by forming such an alliance.

I provided her no such comfort. Instead, I remained guarded in my responses, giving her no satisfaction that her interference had swayed me in any direction. My aunt departed with a huff, leaving me to my thoughts, which were now alight with possibility and determination.

The gravity of this intelligence is not lost on me. Elizabeth's strength of character, her refusal to bow to intimidation, speaks of a depth of feeling I had scarcely allowed myself to hope for. It confirms, in part, what my own heart has known—that there is a bond between us that not even Lady Catherine's formidable will can sever.

As I pen these words, the hour grows late, and the city of London is quiet. Yet within my chest, there is a tumult that rivals the greatest storm. Elizabeth's image fills my mind, her fine eyes alight with that mixture of intellect and fire that first captivated me.

My course is clear. I must return to Hertfordshire, to see Elizabeth, to speak of matters that have been too long relegated to the silence of our hearts. Lady Catherine's intrusion has, perhaps inadvertently, set in motion a series of events that may lead to the most joyous of resolutions.

Until then, I remain in a state of eager anticipation, my thoughts consumed by Elizabeth, and by the future that I dare to envision—one where she stands by my side, not as a specter in my musings, but as my companion, my equal, and my dearest love.

Fitzwilliam Darcy

October 12, 1812

The day dawned with a sense of expectation, for it was to be marked by a visit to Longbourn in the company of my dear friend Bingley. We arrived earlier than anticipated, and I noted the look of momentary dread upon Elizabeth's countenance, fearing we had been informed of Lady Catherine's overbearing visit. Yet, before Mrs. Bennet could address the matter, Bingley, with intentions transparent to us all, proposed a walk. The suggestion was readily accepted, and thus we found ourselves traversing the familiar paths of Hertfordshire.

As fate would ordain, the party soon divided, allowing Bingley and Jane to indulge in the comfort of each other's exclusive company. I was left with Elizabeth and her sister Kitty, who, either by design or happy chance, sought to visit Maria Lucas, granting Elizabeth and me a privacy that was both daunting and desired.

Our conversation was initially sparse, the weight of our shared history hanging between us. It was Elizabeth who broke the silence, her voice carrying the unmistakable timbre of resolve as she began, "Mr. Darcy, I am a very selfish creature, and for the sake of giving relief to my own feelings care not how much I may be wounding yours. I can no longer help thanking you for your unexampled kindness to my poor sister."

Her forthright gratitude, though spoken with a concern for my feelings, was received with a mixture of surprise and emotion. "I am sorry, exceedingly sorry," I replied, "that you have ever been informed of what may, in a mistaken light, have given you uneasiness. I did not think Mrs. Gardiner was so little to be trusted."

"You must not blame my aunt. Lydia's thoughtlessness first betrayed to me that you had been concerned in the matter; and, of course, I could not rest till I knew the particulars. Let me thank you again and again, in the name of all my family, for that generous compassion which induced you to take so much trouble, and bear so many mortifications, for the sake of discovering them."

Our discourse evolved, and I found myself confessing the true impetus behind my actions. "If you will thank me," I said, my gaze steady upon her, "let it be for yourself alone. That the wish of giving happiness to you might add force to the other inducements which led me on, I shall not attempt to deny. But your family owe me nothing. Much as I respect them, I believe I thought only of you."

The admission hung heavily in the air, and I braced myself for her response, which came not in words but in a telling silence that spoke volumes. After a pause, filled with unspoken emotion, I ventured further, laying my heart bare. "You are too generous to trifle with me. If your feelings are still what they were last April, tell me so at once. My affections and wishes are unchanged; but one word from you will silence me on this subject for ever."

Elizabeth, clearly overwhelmed by the gravity of the moment, was not immediate in her reply. Yet, when she spoke, her words conveyed a shift in her sentiments that I had scarcely dared to hope for. "My feelings," she admitted, "are so different now from what they were then, as to be unrecognizable. You must believe me when I say that I am grateful for your affections, and that I return them with a sincerity and warmth that matches your own."

The joy that suffused me upon hearing her avowal was unlike any I had ever known. Our subsequent conversation, as we continued our walk, was a tapestry of earnest declarations and heartfelt admissions. We spoke of our mistakes, our growth, and the light which Lady Catherine's interference had inadvertently cast upon our understanding of each other.

As we neared Longbourn once again, our future lay before us—a future filled with the promise of shared happiness and mutual respect. The task that awaited me was clear: to seek the approval of Mr. Bennet and to begin the journey of a lifetime with the incomparable Elizabeth Bennet by my side.

Today, I approached a task that, in my younger years, I had never imagined would bring such a tumult of emotions—a request for a gentleman's most treasured blessing, the hand of his daughter in marriage. After the revelations shared between Elizabeth and myself, it was imperative that I seek the consent of her father, Mr. Bennet, a man I have come to regard with a mixture of respect and curiosity.

I requested a private audience with him, which he granted with an expression that bore the traces of intrigue. We retreated to his library, a sanctum of quiet dignity, and I found myself momentarily studying the titles that lined the shelves before turning my attention to the matter at hand.

"Mr. Bennet," I began, my voice steady despite the rapid beating of my heart, "I come before you today to express a sentiment which, until very recently, I feared might remain unspoken."

Mr. Bennet leaned back in his chair, his eyes sharp and assessing. "Indeed, Mr. Darcy? And what sentiment might that be?"

"It is one of affection—affection for your second daughter, Miss Elizabeth Bennet." I paused, gathering my thoughts. "I have had the privilege of knowing Miss Elizabeth for some time now, and the esteem I hold for her has grown into a fervent and committed love. I am here to humbly request your permission to ask for her hand in marriage."

Mr. Bennet regarded me with a mixture of surprise and contemplation. After a moment, he responded with a measured tone. "You have my attention, sir, and I must say, this is quite unexpected. My Lizzy is a girl of fine mind and lively spirit. Tell me, Mr. Darcy, are you quite certain of her feelings towards you?"

"Indeed, I am, sir," I replied with confidence. "Miss Elizabeth has honored me with the assurance of her affections, which, I can say with all sincerity, are reciprocated in full measure by my own."

Mr. Bennet nodded, a slight smile touching his lips. "Well, Mr. Darcy, I will not deny that your proposal comes as a surprise, given the... rocky commencement of your acquaintance. However, I have observed a change in both of you, and it would be remiss of me not to acknowledge it."

He paused, a thoughtful expression crossing his face. "Furthermore, I must express my family's gratitude for the role you played in the recent matter of my youngest daughter, Lydia. Your discretion and generosity in that unfortunate affair have not gone unnoticed, and for that, you have my sincerest thanks."

I inclined my head, accepting his gratitude with a sense of duty fulfilled. "Thank you, Mr. Bennet. It was my honor to assist in the matter. The well-being of your daughter was of utmost concern to me, as is the happiness of all your family."

Mr. Bennet's gaze was steady. "And what of your own family, Mr. Darcy? How do they regard this match?"

"My sister, Georgiana, holds Miss Elizabeth in high esteem, and I have no doubt she will be overjoyed by our union. As for my other relations, I am confident they will recognize the wisdom of my choice and the virtue of the lady who has captured my heart."

After a moment of silence, in which the gravity of our discussion seemed to weigh upon the room, Mr. Bennet extended his hand. "Very well, Mr. Darcy. You have my consent to ask Elizabeth to be your wife. I trust you will both seek to make each other deservedly happy."

Grasping his hand firmly, I felt a profound sense of relief and gratitude. "Thank you, sir. I assure you, I shall endeavor to do so with every fiber of my being."

As I left the library, my steps were light, and my future, once shrouded in doubt, now seemed bright with the promise of shared joy.

The path ahead would undoubtedly present its challenges, but with Elizabeth by my side, I felt equipped to face whatever may come.

Fitzwilliam Darcy

October 16, 1812

It is with a lightness of heart that I now sit to recount today's events, a day marked by playful banter and the joy of an attachment freely acknowledged. Elizabeth and I found ourselves in the delightful enterprise of understanding one another more deeply, probing the whimsicalities of our affection with the comfort of a future secured.

As we strolled through the verdant expanse of her father's estate, Elizabeth, ever so teasingly, inquired after the origins of my affection for her. "How could you begin?" she asked with a spirited smile. "I can comprehend your going on charmingly, when you had once made a beginning; but what could set you off in the first place?"

I found myself momentarily at a loss, the precise moment in which my admiration began having long since melded into the tapestry of my constant regard for her. "I cannot fix on the hour, or the spot, or the look, or the words, which laid the foundation," I confessed, my tone reflective. "It is too long ago. I was in the middle before I knew that I had begun."

Her laughter was music to my ears, and she playfully continued her inquiry, pressing me on the nature of my initial resistance to her charms. "My beauty you had early withstood, and as for my manners—my behaviour to you was at least always bordering on the uncivil, and I never spoke to you without rather wishing to give you pain than not. Now, be sincere; did you admire me for my impertinence?"

"For the liveliness of your mind, I did," I answered earnestly, recognizing in her the spark that had so thoroughly captivated me.

Elizabeth chided me, suggesting that what I called liveliness was indeed impertinence, and that my attraction to her was born out of a weariness for those who sought my approval too eagerly. She spoke with a self-assurance that both amused and endeared her further to me. Her theory was that, despite my efforts to appear indifferent, my true feelings—noble and just—had rendered me unable to despise her as others might have in my place.

Our conversation meandered through the events that had brought us together, touching upon the commendable care she had shown towards her sister Jane during her illness at Netherfield. I could not help but praise her for the affection and duty that had shone so brightly in her actions.

Elizabeth, in her characteristic manner, turned my praise into an opportunity for further jest. "My good qualities are under your protection, and you are to exaggerate them as much as possible," she declared. "And in return, it belongs to me to find occasions for teasing and quarrelling with you as often as may be; and I shall begin directly by asking you what made you so unwilling to come to the point at last?"

I admitted to her, "Because you were grave and silent, and gave me no encouragement." Our mutual confessions of embarrassment revealed the common ground of our initial misunderstandings, and we each acknowledged the role that Lady Catherine's misguided interference had played in bringing clarity to our feelings.

As we returned to the house, Elizabeth, with a touch of mischief, asked me to write to Lady Catherine and announce our engagement, an errand I accepted with a sense of duty, albeit not without trepidation. Elizabeth, too, took to her pen with alacrity, eager to share our good news with her aunt and uncle Gardiner, whose own role in our courtship was not insignificant.

The remainder of the day was spent in the company of family, each interaction underscored by the newfound understanding between us. I bore the civilities and occasional vulgarities of our acquaintances with the patience of a man whose every happiness was assured. Elizabeth, ever considerate, endeavored to shield me from discomfort, a gesture that only deepened my admiration for her.

In the midst of society's demands, we found solace in our shared anticipation of a future away from the prying eyes and ears of the world—a future at Pemberley, where the elegance and comfort of family would be ours to enjoy without reserve.

Fitzwilliam Darcy

October 30, 1812

The days have passed in a whirlwind of activity, each moment etching itself into the fabric of my memory. Today, Mrs. Bennet finds herself relieved of the care of her two most deserving daughters, and with what pride she speaks of Mrs. Bingley and myself! One might venture to say that her maternal satisfaction knows no bounds.

It is a curious thing to observe the dynamics of the Bennet household in the wake of such significant changes. Mrs. Bennet's elation, while genuine, has not entirely banished her propensity for silliness, nor has it endowed her with a sudden penchant for wisdom. Mr. Bennet, for his part, seems to have reconciled himself to a quieter household with a bemused resignation, finding solace in his frequent visits to Pemberley. There, I suspect, he delights in the comfort of Elizabeth's company and the tranquility of our grounds.

Meanwhile, Bingley and Jane have taken up residence at Netherfield, though the proximity to Mrs. Bennet and the society of Meryton has proven less than desirable. In an amicable decision, they have chosen to seek a new estate within thirty miles of Pemberley—a move that promises continued closeness between our families.

Kitty, much improved by the influence of her elder sisters, has grown in both temperament and understanding. The absence of Lydia's less commendable example has allowed her to mature into a young lady of more discerning character.

Mary, the last of the Bennet sisters at home, has found herself drawn into society more frequently. With the burden of comparison to her sisters' beauty lifted, she has begun to navigate social engagements with a newfound ease, though her penchant for moralizing remains undiminished.

As for Lydia and Wickham, their existence continues much as it began—unsettled and imprudent. Despite the knowledge of Wickham's character now fully revealed to Elizabeth, I have, for her sake, extended what assistance I can to his career. Lydia, ever vivacious and lacking in self-reflection, visits Pemberley when her husband indulges in his jaunts to London or Bath.

Miss Bingley's initial mortification at my marriage has, in time, given way to a pragmatic acceptance. She maintains her connection to Pemberley and has embraced a renewed affection for Georgiana, as well as a dutiful civility towards Elizabeth.

Georgiana has adapted well to her new role as mistress of Pemberley alongside Elizabeth. The bond between the sisters has blossomed into a genuine and heartfelt attachment. Through Elizabeth's influence, Georgiana is learning the delicate art of sisterly camaraderie—a dynamic quite different from the reverence she once held exclusively for me.

Lady Catherine's indignation at our union has been as vociferous as it was predictable. Yet, in time, even she has been persuaded to visit Pemberley, curiosity perhaps outweighing her objections. Her presence in our home, while initially a source of apprehension, has become a testament to the enduring nature of family ties.

The Gardiners remain our steadfast friends and confidants. Their role in bringing Elizabeth into my life cannot be overstated, and for that, my gratitude is immeasurable.

As I close this entry, I reflect on the intricate web of relationships that now define my world. The joy, love, and occasional trials interwoven within this tapestry of familial ties serve as a constant reminder of the richness of life. Above all, it is Elizabeth who stands at the center of my universe, her love and companionship the greatest of all blessings I have been afforded.

Fitzwilliam Darcy

December 31, 1812

As I sit to pen what shall be the last entry in this particular volume of my journals, I am struck by the profound journey that has unfolded within these pages. From the initial moments of prejudiced views and prideful reticence, to the blossoming of the most ardent love and respect, my transformation has been both humbling and exalting. The narrative of my life has become inextricably linked with that of Elizabeth, and it is a story I shall continue to cherish as we step into the future together.

The year wanes, and with it, the remnants of my former self—the aloof, solitary man who walked the halls of Pemberley with a heart yet untouched by the truest form of companionship. The tapestry of my life before Elizabeth was one of duty and decorum, devoid of the vibrant colors she has woven into it with her wit, her intelligence, and her unguarded affection.

Looking back upon our first encounter, it is with a sense of wonder that I recall the man I was—a man who could not perceive the treasure before him. Elizabeth, with her fine eyes and spirited manner, challenged me, confounded me, and ultimately captured me in a way no other ever had. My admiration for her, once begrudging and concealed, has grown into a love that is as integral to my being as the air I breathe.

In the quiet hours of reflection, I often revisit the pivotal moments that have marked our journey—the misunderstandings at the Meryton assembly, the dance at Netherfield, the tempestuous exchange at Hunsford Parsonage, and the unexpected warmth of our reunion at

Pemberley. Each encounter, whether fraught with tension or filled with understanding, has shaped the man I have become.

The trials we have faced, from the scandal surrounding Lydia to the interference of Lady Catherine, have tested and strengthened our bond. In overcoming these obstacles, we have forged a unity that is fortified by mutual respect and shared values.

Now, as Elizabeth and I stand on the cusp of a new year, I am filled with a sense of eager anticipation for the life we will build together. Pemberley, once a symbol of my lineage and status, has become a home filled with laughter, conversation, and the warmth of familial love. The presence of Jane and Bingley nearby, the improvement of Kitty under our collective care, and the maturation of Mary—all contribute to the joy of our daily existence.

Even as I endeavor to support Wickham in his profession, out of regard for Elizabeth, I do so with the knowledge that the trials he and Lydia face are of their own making. Their presence in our lives is a reminder that family is complex and often imperfect, yet deserving of compassion.

As for Georgiana, who once viewed me with a reverence reserved for elder brothers, she has found in Elizabeth not only a sister but a friend and confidante. Through Elizabeth's gentle guidance, she has begun to emerge from the shadow of timidity, embracing a newfound confidence that is a delight to witness.

In the year to come, I look forward to the continued growth of our family, to moments of shared happiness and private understanding, and to the deepening of the love that has become the cornerstone of my existence.

I close this journal with a heart full of gratitude—for the love that has transformed me, for the trials that have tested me, and for the woman who stands beside me as my wife, my equal, and my dearest friend.

With a hopeful gaze set upon the horizon of our future, I am, now and always,

Fitzwilliam Darcy

THE END

Also by June Calva

Dreamweaver's
Dreamweaver's The Slumbering Key

Standalone
Southern Shadows' Veil's of Twilight
The Collector
The Lost Journal's of Fitzwilliam Darcy

Watch for more at https://msha.ke/junecalva.

About the Author

I am a passionate author, exploring various genres that range from historical romance to supernatural thrillers. Writing has not only sharpened my skills but has also helped me discover my true self.

Read more at https://msha.ke/junecalva.